Leaving the Neighborhood
and Other Stories

Also by Lucy Ferriss

<u>Novels</u>
The Misconceiver
Against Gravity
The Gated River
Philip's Girl

<u>Literary Criticism</u>
Sleeping with the Boss:
Female Subjectivity and Narrative Pattern in Robert Penn Warren

Lucy Ferriss

LEAVING THE NEIGHBORHOOD

AND OTHER STORIES

Mid-List Press
Minneapolis

FIRST SERIES: SHORT FICTION

Published by Mid-List Press, 4324 12th Avenue South, Minneapolis, Minnesota 55407-3218. Visit our website at www.midlist.org.

First printing: June 2001
04 03 02 01   7 6 5 4 3 2 1

Printed in the United States of America

Library of Congress Cataloging-in-Publication Data
Ferriss, Lucy, 1954-
    Leaving the neighborhood and other stories / Lucy Ferriss.
    p. cm.
    "First Series: short fiction"
    Contents: The vortex—Stampede—Bones—Leaving the neighborhood—Rumplestiltskin—Mud time—Politics—Husband material—Safe-T-Man—Time share—Purring—The woman who said no.
    ISBN 0-922811-50-4 (trade paper : alk. paper)
    1. United States—Social life and customs—20th century—Fiction. I. Title
PS3556.E754 L4 2001
813'.54—dc21   2001030173

Cover Art: Charcoal drawing by Lawrence Ferlinghetti
Cover and text design: Lane Stiles

Grateful acknowledgment is made to the following journals where these stories, sometimes in slightly different form, first appeared: *American Literary Review*, "Stampede"; *Massachusetts Review*, "Bones"; *River City*, "Leaving the Neighborhood"; *Louisville Review*, "Rumpelstiltskin"; *Carolina Quarterly*, "Safe-T-Man"; *Shenandoah*, "Time-Share"; *Missouri Review*, "The Woman Who Said No."

Acknowledgments

These stories exist individually and as a collection through the gallant friendship and unflagging support of their first readers and editors: Mark P. Couzens, William J. Cobb, Molly Giles, Rose Ann Miller, Kevin Prufer, Juliet Woulfe, Eric Goodman, Speer Morgan, R.T. Smith, Julia Demmin, Barbara Rodman, Shannon Wooden, Mary Lee Settle, Stuart Dybek, George Core, Marianne Leslie Nora, Lisa Birnbaum, and Lane Stiles. To these readers and to those listed with some of these stories, this book is dedicated.

For the time and space in which these stories germinated and grew, I am indebted to the Corporation of Yaddo, the Virginia Center for the Creative Arts, the faculty development fund of Hamilton College, and the patience of my children, Luke and Daniel Couzens.

Contents

The Vortex

For M.B.

As he wakes, he hears her in the kitchen, starting coffee. The mewl of her cats, radio turned on low. If she comes back to the bed, he'll want to make love to her again. He doesn't raise himself up, quite yet. If she comes back, maybe with a cup of coffee for him, she'll be wearing that robe she used to wear, with the wood ducks on it, and she'll move her body over his like a cat stretching its hindquarters.

His clothes hang over the back of her small chair, in the corner. Jacket and tie: he was attending a conference, that was why he came to this city. As he turns toward the half-open window her sheets slide over his naked buttocks, cool and smooth. He shakes a cigarette from the pack he left on her nightstand and lights it. Outside it's foggy—this is the part of the city that stays foggy much of the time, he remembers. He went to graduate school here. You can smell the salt air. What street did she say she lived on? Thirty-ninth—eleven blocks, then, from the water.

Sure enough, she comes in, with the coffee. "You drink it black, right?" she says. "You used to drink it black."

"Excellent memory." He takes the mug from her and puts it on the side table. She's not wearing the duck robe. An oversized T-shirt hangs off her thin shoulders; her wavy hair is wet from the shower.

"Come here," he says. How nervous she acts! Taking the cigarette from his hand the way she used to, dragging on it, scarcely inhaling. Her cork-brown irises quiver. Last night, he remembers now, she started chattering about books she'd read, about nineteenth-century opera; he could hardly focus on the words that came spilling out of her mouth before he stopped her mouth with his.

"I want to be in you," he says, after he's tasted the coffee, "one more time. Before I have to go. Can we do that?"

"Oh, yes," she says, and pulls back the sheet. She puts her mouth on him. The pleasure astonishes; before, she'd been shy, afraid of hurting him. Being married has taught her a thing or two. She's still too thin, her breasts like soft pods on her chest. In the morning light, her freckles show reddish, all down her arms and thighs. "I've got breakfast for you," she says as he enters her, as if she's trying to be a good wife.

"Yes," he says, "and it is delicious."

She wants him truly, now, just when it is too late and she can do nothing but giggle and play around. Before, only he was married; now they both are. Though she's explained to him about Jeremy, how Jeremy's gone off to study in Japan for three months. Maybe because he's accustomed to being her lover, this news does not lead him to questions; her spending the night with him in no way warns him that she's burned out on this marriage. Well, good. She doesn't want to scare him off. She wants only to feel desired, to taste the edge of passion. Now, perhaps, it is she who is using him.

Though, even now, he won't take her seriously. There she was trying to talk about her thesis for Christ's sake, and she could see his eyes watching her lips, as if the name Gustav Mahler were some kind of sexual innuendo. Is there nothing new she can tell him, or do lovers simply not talk? She talks plenty, with Jeremy, but they are not lovers any more.

Only one egg in the refrigerator, she discovered just now, and barely enough milk, going bad, and no cereal or bread.

She'll have to make pancakes with one egg—they don't taste so good that way—and there's only marmalade to top them with. She's self-conscious about her cooking, about what she can whip up in the kitchen on a moment's notice. She's never cooked for her lover before. It ought to be lovely. Fluffy omelets and fresh-squeezed orange juice, real cream for the coffee even if he doesn't take it. He's moving in her now, and she catches her breath, then exhales close to his naked chest. Turning her onto her back, he loops her legs over his shoulders—she can still do that, flexible from dance—and he plunges deeper, and she thinks *fuck fuck fucking*, maybe she says it even.

When he was kissing her in the cab, on the way over, he'd slipped for a minute outside time, and it was a younger self kissing a young woman in a cab in New York City, driving through the rain. What good fortune he's had, in his life! To see her eyes shine like that, little half-moons in the irises reflecting the street lamps as they sped over Twin Peaks, so happy she was to learn that he could really spend the night. Well, of course he could—he'd have been at his hotel room otherwise, and his wife knowing full well he stayed out late at these conferences, he always has.

She'd told him her husband was in Japan, studying—what? Zen Buddhism maybe, some nonsense. "Last time we saw each other," he reminded her—stroking her hair, loose from its clip now, cool against the cab seat—"you pushed me away because you were going to marry him. Remember?"

"I do, I do. You'd made it as far as my bedroom, that waterbed. You said you wanted to try it out."

"You still have that bed?"

"No. Jeremy said it made him seasick."

"We missed that opportunity, then."

"Oh, I'm sorry." She looked sorry, the silly thing, stroking his neck. "I liked that bed, too."

He'd known she would not be a faithful wife. Not because there was anything wrong with this Jeremy—he'd met him, finally, a tall serious young man, too mystical for his taste—but because she would always need more than marriage could give her. The fare to the Sunset District shocked her. "You never take cabs?" he asked, and she shook her head, bashful. She went ahead of him, up the stairs to her little row house. He liked watching her fumble with her keys, greet the cat on her way in, check the answering machine—all those little signs that said she was older, she had a life; she was a woman he could love and not feel responsible for.

"I have bourbon," she said when she'd fed the cat, and he nodded, reaching for her.

If only the cab ride could have lasted forever. The lights flying by, and him kissing her like that. She was so wet on her panties it was embarrassing. Nothing so private as a cab, even with the driver in the front and all the other cars passing by. That dark, familiar space, with so much legroom! And the way they spoke to one another, in voices just above whispers. "You never told me this was your stomping ground," she said.

"Well, Berkeley."

"I wish I lived on that side of the bay. Gets so *foggy*, out here. It depresses me."

"I'm glad you came and found me."

"I didn't know if I'd find you there. I couldn't resist going. With Jeremy out of town, you know."

"This feels good."

"Can you stay? Can you stay the night?"

"Of course I can." His broad face, always laughing a little at her. But he wasn't so scary, in the cab—and she'd always been a little scared of him, all that year in L.A., as if he would suddenly disapprove of her or be disappointed in her. Here he was a middle-aged guy at an out-of-town conference, pleased as punch to be riding home with a girl instead of stuck at that hotel with its sterile rooms. Which was actually how she'd pictured them, in one of those soft double beds with the fake brocade coverlets. It had been his idea to come out to her place. And so she let him pay for the cab, none of this Dutch-treat business she used to insist on, it was her home they were going to, her marriage bed. As the cab pulled onto Thirty-Ninth she kissed his neck a last time, flicking her tongue over the delicate skin there, as if she would never love him more than in that dingy car.

It was one thing he'd taught himself—to ride the waves of life lightly, take what good fortune brings along. Certainly it was a shift of gears—he'd been planning on a poker game, later, with a bunch of guys from Seattle and Vancouver that he hadn't seen in two years—but he quickly switched to squiring her around the reception at the hotel, introducing her to people he knew to be either discreet or thickheaded. He'd given his paper just before this reception, and it had been well received. Once he'd got her a drink, and they'd made the rounds, he found himself talking to her about the conference, just as if they'd planned to meet here, as if they'd been in touch all this while. "Do you know, a young guy grabbed me, on the way out of the hall just now, and pumped my hand, and I guess he was impressed, he said, 'Wow, John Stehlman, I thought you were *dead.*'"

"Dead!" She put the back of her hand to her mouth, shocked.

"I don't think he meant as in *old*. I think he meant as in *famous*—you know, as if Philip Glass had just walked through the door, here. It gave me a little glimpse of my rep beyond the tomb."

He blew smoke out through his nostrils, and she reached her hand for the cigarette. She never had her own—it was a kind of flirtation for her, smoking his cigarettes. He wasn't one to mind. Above them hung the huge crystal chandelier of the hotel's main ballroom, a gaudy throwback to days, long before this hotel was built, when there were balls and gas lighting, the prisms of the chandelier refracting and enlarging the tiny flames. Now people—men, mostly, some middle-aged women, a few earnest graduate students—simply milled around, getting quietly drunk. No one else like her in the room; she might have been a great sunflower brought in from the country to shame all the silk arrangements.

"Have you had dinner?" he asked her, being polite.

"Dinner!" she said, dipping another shrimp from the huge pink pile into the hot sauce on the hors d'oeuvres table. "*This* is dinner."

That was when he knew it would be all right, he could ride this wave—and he felt it, that place in his heart he'd closed off when she left, opening like a valve.

Someday, she thought at the reception, when they were no longer lovers, she would be able to tell him what she'd always appreciated about him: the way he could take your most ridiculous action and turn it into something natural, something he was glad you'd done. Long ago, when she lived five blocks from his solid adobe house with its playset in the back yard and potted plants in the mudroom, she sometimes skulked around at night, peeking in his windows, just to understand this life of his from which she was excluded. She'd seen his wife put the dinner dishes away; watched his teenaged son slouch in front of the TV set in the den; caught a glimpse of him picking up the phone, putting on his glasses to check a note he'd made. Once, after midnight, when she couldn't stand it any more, she'd tapped on the glass of his study, and he'd come out to the front porch and shared a cigarette with her. *I'm so glad you came!* he kept saying, even though it was a stupid risk, an intrusion.

Likewise, this conference reception, where she stuck out like a weed—too pretty a dress, plus her perfume, and everyone at the conference seemed to know one another besides. The sensible thing would have been to leave him a message at the reception desk. But now he acted as if she were a celebrity who'd deigned to drop in. His hand at the small of her back, he introduced her to middle-aged men who asked what work she did, how long she'd been in the city. Until, in a hiatus of conversation, out of earshot of the others, he asked her plans for the evening, and she told him Jeremy was out of the country. His grin unbalanced his face; he tipped his head as if listening. Noticing the extra gray in his hair, around the ears, she thought for the first time how this was all about sex, the way life is all about food and water. She tasted his lips on the filter of his cigarette.

Before he saw her, that evening, he had been caught up in a discussion of artificial intelligence, based on the Kasparov chess game. His end of the argument had to do with memory, on which he argued the human brain relied very little; there were certain functions, no doubt, in which greater memory capacity would help a being to perform better, but we were a long way from equating intelligence and memory. He'd cited Einstein as an example and been routed by a young computer expert who claimed Einstein could have unlocked far more mysteries of the universe if he had had more memory. "What's more, we have yet to determine the extent to which memory does figure in our calculations," the young man went on. "What may be missing is our capacity to locate the memory *function*, because the brain operates more efficiently by moving *forward*."

"Look, I'm the first to admit that the idea of Kasparov operating by so-called intuition is a crock," he'd said. "But isn't it possible that the use of chess as an assessment of intelligence is useful only insofar as it isn't assessing memory instead?"

"Don't let Stehlman fool you," one of his old colleagues had put in, leaning into the young man. "He doesn't even *play* chess."

Which was true. He preferred poker, blackjack, all games of chance. Still, this discussion of memory unnerved him. He was a philosopher of mind; he considered himself a fringe participant in the artificial-intelligence discussion. Memory was a golem, not a collection of bits.

And then he saw her. Straight out of his past, only more beautiful because self-possessed. She was wearing a yellow dress, perfect for the warm May day that shone outside—you forgot the season, in these climate-controlled hotels. On her narrow feet, white sandals; on her head the hair piled loosely, the way she used to wear it in the heat. She ran up a couple of steps of the long, winding staircase that went down to the main lobby; then she slowed down and mounted pensively, then skipped again. Surely it's a coincidence, he thought. She lives in this city now, this is a big hotel, perhaps she has business here. Her hand glided up the rail as she climbed the stairs, those strong pianist's fingers stroking the brass. Twenty-five, she must be now, he thought, and married. Never once had he told her that he loved her. Now they would greet each other with surprise, and she would go on to whatever business she had.

And then she looked up, to where he was leaning over the balcony, and when she smiled he knew that she had found him, that she had in fact come looking for him, and swallowing his bourbon he moved toward her.

Absurd, she'd been telling herself from noon onward. Frivolous and absurd, to waste a whole afternoon preparing to see a man you used to see almost every day. It was fantasy, that was all. Since marrying Jeremy she had learned a lot about fantasy. How good it was to indulge in, how dangerous to believe in. She had fantasized about the men in her graduate classes, the father of one of the children she taught, the work-booted guy who ran a leather shop around the corner from the row house she rented with Jeremy. She wasn't ready to think about why she had chained herself to Jeremy, who had wanted her so much at first and now hardly at all. How easy it had been, to see him leave for a few months! Perhaps, if he left frequently, she would find a way to survive this; she would become married truly and not just in name. Meanwhile, her fantasy centered on the poster she'd seen on the graduate bulletin board, the one with a drawing of the brain overlaid by silicon chips, advertising an artificial-intelligence conference, speakers from all over the country, neurologists and philosophers of mind, the whole gamut. John Stehlman, she'd thought, John Stehlman would have to be there, he's always being asked to speak at these things, he'll be at that hotel downtown and I can surprise the daylights out of him.

Of course it was fantasy. His name wasn't on the poster. No reason he should even be at such a conference; if he were, no way she would find him in the swarm of people, such a big hotel. If she called first. But no, she was ready to be disappointed, she only wanted to spend the afternoon washing her hair, rubbing lotion and powder into her skin, shaving her legs that she hadn't bothered with since before Jeremy left. Already she'd gone around the corner to the liquor shop for a bottle of good bourbon—Jeremy wouldn't drink alcohol at all, he was so staid. She wouldn't bring it with her, that would be a bad omen. If they ended up in his hotel room, he'd have brought his own bourbon; this was for here, in case he was sharing his room or just wanted to visit. If she had no luck finding him—and she wouldn't have luck, this was fantasy—she'd just drink it herself, a shot every night until Jeremy came home. She put on makeup, and those earrings he'd brought her back from Mexico, and Chanel No. 5 that he'd asked about, the first time they had met. In a little while she would take the streetcar downtown and he would not be there. She would heave a great sigh, there in the lobby of the hotel, and maybe to compensate she would take herself out to dinner. She would tell herself, late that night when the cat climbed into her lap, that it was far better to keep the past in the past.

Still, so much time to spend on oneself! The yellow dress, too, was an indulgence, but she liked how the skirt swirled around her knees, how the bodice fit her small chest. Perhaps it was worth it, she thought as she stepped off the streetcar onto the warm pavement of early evening—worth it to make oneself beautiful from time to time, even when there was no one there to reflect it. It made her happy to think about him. To think how he had let her go, when she needed to go into the world and make a life for herself. How he had sent her a poem, once, a silly thing, and she had not responded because she was marrying Jeremy; and then he came and found her, in that silly apartment in L.A., and he kissed her and fondled her breasts on the waterbed. As she breezed into the hotel she was thinking how he used to touch her, always with a trace of sadness. Oh, I am yours, I am yours! she indulged herself in shouting, wrapped in anticipation, nothing would come of it. She was halfway up the stairs, smiling at her fond fantasy, when a sound from above roused her, and she looked up into his familiar face.

Stampede

She had thought he might be the same man, though the first name didn't ring a bell. Even if he were, she had plenty to take care of, with introducing the speaker and making sure Mrs. Lederle sat at the head table and steering Judson away from the bar. So what if she knew him? He wouldn't know her.

Ah, but he did. Still tall and lean but a little heavy toward the middle now, he glanced Elissa's way while she shook hands with three or four visiting research people. Tapping her notes into place, she could feel his eyes on her. She never thought she'd be doing this, helping host a dinner for the Leukemia Foundation. It was the sort of role she used to picture society types in; she was a worker, a politically conscious person, a freak emeritus. Well, she gave the intro anyhow. After the guy's speech, there was stand-up dessert.

"Elissa?" he said, from just a little too far away so people turned to find the voice.

"Oh," she said, drawing her eyebrows down as if she were straining to recognize, "Sandy? Sandy Martin? Or is it still Sandy now?"

He'd cropped his hair close, so the gold curls hugged tight like one of those men's perms. His smile spread across his face as he moved toward her. "Still Sandy," he said, and took her hand in his firm one.

"What do you know," she said, letting him kiss her cheek

and thinking, *You dumb fucking jerk.*

He wrote down her number and soon called, so they had lunch. Of course he looked beefier than he had in college. Who didn't? On the other hand, the laugh lines cutting down his cheeks added angles where there had been curves, and drew attention to the sweep of his mouth. Every now and then he winced, as if recalling a painful moment. He showed her snaps of his yellow-haired kids, just older than hers, boy and girl. She ended up admitting she'd thought he was in town—"There was your picture in the paper, you know, when you joined the CDC. It said Jay Sanford Martin, but it looked like the same you."

"Not hardly. I'd just got back from Kenya." He named the country offhandedly, used to exotic parts. "I'd dropped thirty pounds."

"Well."

She showed him snaps of Judson and their daughter Mary Lee, and told him about Michael. "It was only three months, and we knew from the start. I guess I didn't think it would sock me the way it did." She watched him shake his head; he'd heard this sort of thing before. "So when they called from the Foundation, I was putty in their hands."

"You raised a fair amount at that dinner, I bet."

"Almost twenty thou. How are you liking Atlanta?"

"Wrong ocean, but it's a fun town."

"That's what they tell me," said Elissa, aware that she sounded a little snide, a little smug, as if her tragedy gave her a right. They ordered and sipped at white wine. She got him to talk about his job, mostly reports and publications. "You knew I was premed," he reminded her, though she hadn't; but he'd never finished the M.D., had gone into the quantitative end instead. And then Africa, twelve years, where he'd met his beautiful Aussie wife who'd stayed over there.

"You were always the golden boy," she said, out of nowhere.

He winced. "Those were wild days."

"I guess." They ducked their heads toward their wine glasses, then looked up: a conspiring smile. "You had that incredible mass of blond curls," Elissa went on. "And I remember I was going out with that preppy guy Frank when I first met you, and later I found out you'd gone to school together."

"Yeah, Frank," Sandy said. He broke off a hunk of French bread and buttered it. He still had those big bony hands, Elissa noticed, and she flashed on his fingers rolling a row of joints in the predawn light. "Wonder what happened to ole Frank."

"I think he married that girl who played star tennis."

"Yeah, he would."

Elissa stole a peek at her watch, below the tablecloth. She'd rescheduled the one o'clock but still had a client at two. "I was so amazed to find out you were a boarding-school boy."

"Takes all kinds." But he looked just a little uncomfortable; the bread stopped halfway to his mouth.

"I mean, none of us really thought about where you'd come from. You were this tall blond hippie God, and we followed you."

"That's kind of an exaggeration, don't you think?"

"No, really. When you weren't around, it was always 'Sandy told me this,' or 'Sandy did that.' Knowing Sandy more or less got you into the crowd. I was grateful to Frank for that, even after we broke up and he went the jock route. I became someone who knew Sandy. Even though you didn't know me." She was spilling, she hated people who spilled but who else would care about the Sandy thing nowadays except Sandy?

"I did know you!" he protested.

She tipped her head, hand to chin. "But you knew everybody. The women were all crazy about you. Which was why—I figured—you kept it quiet about who you were sleeping with at any given time. To keep us all guessing and ready."

He was blushing, now, the still-fair skin a little mottled at the throat. "You ladies discussed this?"

"No, never. We were into unisex, remember? No all-girl klatches. It was just something you sensed."

The food came. Broiled salmon for him, pasta salad for her. "Well," he said, looking at his plate as if it were a deep pond. "The invincible days of youth." *brvf*

A few days later she saw him again—funny, how you don't see people in Atlanta for months, and then suddenly they're everywhere. At Home Shopping Barn, where she'd gone for a wicker hamper, Sandy seemed to be buying out the store. Lamp fixtures and shelving, mostly, she noticed; thankfully, no Korean-manufacture mugs, he must still stock the hand-thrown variety.

"Settled into some digs," he said. He was beginning to look more like the Sandy she remembered—something about the way he drove his metal cart down the aisle, that long-legged lope. Still attractive, in spite of the years and her lowered opinion. "Out toward Athens, in the country. You'll have to come visit."

"We're talking a house?"

"Old peach orchard. Pretty much scrub land now, and a dilapidated place I'm going to fix up, weekends. Sort of like— hey, you'll remember!—that farm the college owned, where we used to go on botany weekends. You were a botany major, weren't you?"

"Psych. But I spent time out there. You took me out with a bunch in your van once."

He looked at her as if he were trying to place her face. "Don't remember."

"I wouldn't expect you to. There were a lot of us."

"Look," he said, rummaging in corduroy pockets. "Here's my new phone number. Call me if you're out by the eastern end of the city, I'll give you directions. Or call me at work. Here," and he pulled out a business card, maroon on ivory. "Gets lonely out there," he said, with a nervous twitch. Elissa shoved the pieces of paper in her handbag. The only reason ever to call Sandy would be to get down to it, and she didn't think it was worth getting down to after all these years. Besides, she was feeling a pull toward the man in front of her, here and now. She waited for him while he checked out, and he touched her elbow before they split off in the parking lot.

A few weeks later Judson flew north. Elissa was used to her husband's restlessness. Every six months or so Judson would announce he couldn't stand the South another second, it was being in this frigging backwards bigoted society that made him drink, the people who paid him were lobotomized rednecks, and he'd quit whatever profitable gig he had going at the time and head up to visit his brother Caleb in White Plains, New York, where he was sure the pickings were fatter.

"Caleb's working on a book with this megawatt diet doctor," he said, this time. "They're opening a new clinic in Katonah, which is a really wealthy community, and they want someone to start a marketing campaign. Not just for that clinic; for all of them. Caleb's getting two hundred grand just to ghost the book, so you know there's money in it."

"Go," Elissa said. "You won't rest till you find out."

"Just for a week or so. This promotion thing I'm doing at Cox Cable's a crock, anyhow. They just told me they won't pay the second installment till they see the print ads."

"Don't run out on the money, Judson."

"I've got a *contract*, honey. Only the bastards tie my hands. Make the Yankee work."

"Go," she said again, and he went. Elissa always thought of her husband, at these times, as flying north—he did fly, in an airplane, but she saw him as a migrating bird, acting on instinct. And oh, what a letdown and a relief when he was gone, her foiled prodigy, the kind of man she was doomed to marry and be faithful to.

"C'mon," she said to Mary Lee the first night he was gone, "let's do Chinese."

So mother and daughter went to Won Ton Don Wong, the way they always did, and Mary Lee told Elissa about the boy she was in love with who wouldn't even look at her because of the braces and her big nose. "I'm the ugliest girl in fifth grade," Mary Lee said, picking up her dumpling by hand and dipping it in duck sauce.

"No you're not. Rosie McPeters is uglier. She's fat."

"Okay, the second ugliest."

"When you are twenty-two," said Elissa, aiming a chopstick at her daughter, casting the spell, "you will be beautiful and regretting it."

"What I'll be regretting is that it's too late for everything, by then," said Mary Lee.

That was Friday. Saturday, Mary Lee announced she was spending the night at her friend Amanda's house; Sunday morning she called to say they were going to Amanda's older sister's horse show, she'd need to be picked up by four. Elissa thought maybe she should drive down to the Leukemia Foundation headquarters, where she'd promised to sort through networking letters. And the HQ was on the east side of town, so there she was, earlier than people considered polite on Sundays, putting in a call to old Sandy.

"Elissa Jameson," she reminded him—thinking how it was just the way it had been in college, he barely knew her last name.

"Well, great," he said. "Perfect timing. I've just laid in the patio, we can sit out and have a beer and watch the peaches ripen."

There, in the doorway of his rundown estate, in jeans and white T-shirt, and his hair grown out a little, he really looked like the one she'd known so long ago. And only a month back she'd thought him a stranger! As she came up the walk he held out his hand with a lit joint. "Have a toke," he said. "You're in the country."

Elissa took it and stepped past the half-hung door into the dark cool of the house. "Mm," she said, dragging on the stick. It had been a long time since she'd smoked weed—no one at work admitted to it, and Judson's crowd were all former frat boys, drinkers. "Helluva place you've got here," she said.

The paint on the outside, she'd noticed, had been flaking into white stains on the ground; here inside, pastel wallpaper was peeling from the old plaster walls. "Plenty to keep me occupied," said Sandy. He'd come up behind her, and she was conscious of how tall he was; his chest brushed her left shoulder. "Let me show you in here," he said, putting a hand on that shoulder to steer her past the boxes and plywood and covered furniture into the next room. "This'll be my home office," he said. "Here, finish this, hm?" He handed her the roach and went to throw open a filthy set of curtains. "View of the new patio, the orchard. Sunsets are magnificent."

"Yeah," said Elissa. She went to the bay window he'd unveiled. Just outside, the red bricks were hunkering down in their geometric pattern—*Sandy's handy*, she thought, and almost giggled. It was the dope, changing her. "I could work here," she said with an effort.

"Anytime you like."

"No, I meant in theory. Not practice. It's your place."

The view would be magnificent, later, as the sun descended over a far hill where horses made peg-shapes on the pasture. She turned her eyes away and looked around the room. He'd done a lot more here than in the other room. There was a whole computer setup, a pair of newish sofas, a bulletin board with various notices tacked to it, a lineup of African masks along one wall, a bookshelf. Elissa walked over to the bookshelf and looked at the framed photos set up on its top. "This is your ex, right?" she asked.

"Winifred, yes."

"What happened with the two of you?"

"What usually happens." He stepped over to where she stood, just three or four long steps. "We annoyed the hell out of each other."

"She looks like Margaret Adler. You know, that woman who played the zither, at college. I think you were an item with her for a while, weren't you?"

"Yeah." His eyes crinkled. "Margaret," he said. Then he straightened and looked around the room. "So, this place remind you of that farm, or what?"

"Yeah," Elissa admitted. "Only there was a lot less furniture in that place. More room for sleeping bags." The last few words almost strangled in her throat as she spoke them, but Sandy didn't seem to notice.

"Here," he said, taking her hand naturally, the way the old Sandy always did, "come upstairs."

There were just two bedrooms, identically gabled, one with an old four-poster and the other empty. "I'll fix that up for my kids," Sandy said, "when they come. But check out the light in here."

When Elissa sat on the bed she knew he'd sit next to her, following her eyes out the dust-streaked window. He was getting ready to make his pass, she could feel it. The hair on her arms had gone prickly, and she couldn't seem to let her breath all the way out. Outside the window, birds chattered. Inside there were just the two of them, no one to watch or listen. And so she started talking real slowly, to give him time. "No pigs here," she said.

"'Course not. I told you, it was an orchard."

"But I mean like on that farm the college owned. There were wild pigs there. They stampeded."

"Oh, yeah." He propped a foot up on the windowsill and leaned back. "The only large horde here," he gestured out toward the peach trees, "is stationary."

"I remember," Elissa went on, noticing a female cardinal building her nest in the tree just outside, "the night you picked me up, to go out to that place."

"Yeah? I don't remember."

"'Course you don't. You were going to come by early in the morning, but then Kurt or someone called me around midnight and said, 'Sandy's starting out now. If you're coming, get your stuff together, we'll pick you up.' So of course I sprang to it. I mean, I hadn't even been sure I'd get to go in your van, I thought it was for the more select crowd."

"That was a junkheap of a van," Sandy said.

"I remember we got to the farm around five in the morning," Elissa said.

Sandy pulled another joint out of his T-shirt pocket and lit it. He seemed to be giving her his whole attention. That was, she decided even as she went on talking, the magnet at his center. Had always been. How he just turned himself inside out and seemed to be all there for whatever the person right there and then had to say. She couldn't remember Sandy himself ever speaking a word.

"You know," she said, interrupting her own story, "*you* should have gone into psychotherapy, not me. Oh, I don't mean therapy for *you*," she added when his fine mouth frowned. "I mean as in you would have made a good therapist. Because you listen well, or else you fake it well."

"Kiss me," he said, and without waiting he put his warm hand against her jaw and kissed her mouth. And while part of her stiffened—*you dumb fucking jerk*, she thought, *you jerk*—the stoned part of her enjoyed the warm wet sensation, as he gently pushed her back until they were both lying on the bed. Then, while he let her mouth go and his hands, hesitant, began to stray, she started talking again. A little more quickly, now, as if she didn't have much time.

"It was March," she said, while Sandy's hand drifted over her blouse, "so still dark outside. You'd driven the whole time. I can still see that light halo of your hair the way it looked from back in the van, against the glow of headlights. And I thought we'd all crash, you know, what with the dope we'd smoked the whole way and the hour. But you wanted to stay up. 'We'll see the sun rise over Mount Diablo,' you said. 'C'mon, hurry, or we'll miss it.' So all these people who'd gotten there the night before, plus all of us who'd come up in the van, we followed you in the freezing wind out of the cozy farmhouse through the fields and over the far rise toward the east."

"I kind of remember the sunrise," said Sandy. His hand was wanting to get at her breast; she held his palm there, over her blouse, not yet refusing but not letting him in, not until she stopped talking.

"We all sat there on the far side of the rise and drank Ripple and watched it. After you'd rolled some J's you were completely silent, and I watched you and felt like you were sucking up the sun's early rays, like you were some kind of sun-priest and none of us could ever understand."

"I was," said Sandy. He nuzzled her neck. "I made wax wings, later."

"I don't remember much of the rest of that day," said Elissa. "There were a lot of earth-woman types in the kitchen making breads and veggie casseroles, and some people dropped acid— you might have dropped—and the rest of us smoked pot and ate whatever was around. Maybe I managed to nap in a field somewhere. But mostly I was feeling out of it. I spent a long time up in a tree, reading Hermann Hesse." She couldn't suppress a low, ironic laugh at that one, which Sandy took as a signal to tuck his hand under the blouse. She let him this time, her nipple going erect at the touch. "That evening some guys brought out guitars," she said, "and sang Grateful Dead tunes. I went for a long walk down to the farm entrance, and on the way back I heard a low thundering sound, and I looked to where it was coming from, and I saw all these dark shapes moving fast, over the hill, toward me."

"The wild pigs!"

"Yeah. You remember that?"

"No, they never rushed at me. But the biology department caught and dissected one once."

"But you don't remember how I ran back to tell people I'd almost gotten trampled."

"Hey, you might have."

"They came within a few feet of me. I could smell them, I can still smell them in my mind. This dark, bitter smell—blood and shit, I guess. They were like blind, charging. They weren't going to stop. It freaked me out. I ran all the way back to the house, kind of messed up the mellow evening."

"We probably didn't even notice. If you're talking the weekend I think you're talking, there must've been thirty-five freaks at that place."

"Yeah, well, some noticed. They got me a joint and some wine, calmed me down. By then it was late, and people were lining up for the bathroom. I was practically last in line, and then—I don't know—I must have left my sleeping bag in your van or something, anyway, everybody was already bedded down by the time I was ready to look for a spot. The living room, the dining room, even the kitchen was solid people, racked out on the floor."

"We should do that here sometime." He unbuttoned her blouse. "Peach orchard love-in."

She could tell he wanted her to stop talking. "Anyhow, I finally found a narrow bit of wood floor. It was next to you, sort of. I mean, my feet were between two other people, but my head was about at your waist height. And I was exhausted, with the night before and the adrenaline rush from the stampede. I could hear everyone in the room, breathing. And I thought I'd just match my breath to that breath and go to sleep."

"Sleep would be okay."

"But then there was this zipping sound next to me, and the next thing I knew there was something bumping up against my face. Against my chin, my mouth, my nose."

"Mmm." He hadn't managed to get below the waist of her jeans, and Elissa could tell he'd stopped making an effort to seem as though he was listening. She smelled the tang of his sweat as he drew himself closer in. "Wha' was it?"

"It was your penis, Sandy."

"What?" He stopped moving his hand. Then he raised himself on his elbow and looked at her face. "No," he said.

"Yeah, it was. Oh, I'm sure you didn't know it was me. I mean, I don't think you cared who it was. Except you knew it wasn't a guy. I don't think you were ever into guys."

"Jesus Christ, Elissa, what are you *saying?*" He was pissed. She heard the gall in his voice. She was ruining his afternoon. But she couldn't stop.

"You leaned down," she said, "and spoke to the top of my head, there in the sleeping bag. You said, 'Your mouth. Take it in your mouth.' I didn't want to. I was so tired, and all that wine had made me thirsty. But I could hear all those people, with us there on the floor, breathing, and I knew a lot of them weren't asleep yet. I mean, I'd just lain down, for Chrissake."

"You're making this up."

"I'm *not.* So I took it in my mouth, and it seemed just huge, and so rigid, pressing against the roof of my mouth. One thing you couldn't have known was that I'd never blown a guy before, but I'm not sure that would have helped. The angle was all wrong, for one thing, plus I was too self-conscious. So after a minute you whispered, to the top of my head again, 'Suck it, dammit!' And I tried. I tried until tears were coming out of my eyes, but I felt like I was going to choke on the thing, like I didn't have any saliva left. Believe me, Sandy, all I wanted was to get it over with, so all those people would stop listening to us and go to sleep. But I couldn't."

She stopped for a minute. She'd thought she was going to spill it, right through to the end, but the memory was catching her up, her mouth had gone dry. He'd pulled away, just slightly, there on the bed. She didn't turn to him, but she could tell he was looking away from her, out the window. Half-exposed, her chest felt cold.

"And then?" he asked, his voice like lead.

"Then ... you reached down with your big hand, and you ... and you grabbed my mouth and cheeks, and you ... you sort of pumped them. I thought I was going to suffocate. Because I'd started crying, like I said, and so my nose had clogged up, and now with your hand on me like that, and your dick filling my mouth and ramming at my throat, well, I couldn't breathe at all. I must have started to pass out, because I remember thinking, I'll die like this. The next thing I knew you were gone and there was semen dripping out of my mouth, onto the sleeping bag. I swallowed what I could. I was so scared, you know. So embarrassed. Then I didn't move, the rest of the night. I didn't sleep and I didn't move. I just touched my lips, sometimes, with my own fingers"—she did it, now, as she spoke—"to make sure it was all still there, all my own mouth, not something ripped or ragged or gone rotten. Then in the morning we all got up, and you were no different than you'd ever been."

Sandy was sitting on the edge of the bed, now. Elissa straightened up, as well, and began buttoning her blouse. When she was done, she went to the window and looked down on the patio. "I've always wanted," she said after a long while, "to tell you that was me. That girl whose mouth you came in at the farm. It was me, Sandy. Elissa."

From the bed he looked up at her. He held a joint in his hand, but he didn't light it. The pain in his blue eyes was gone; they looked hollow, like he hadn't slept or was hung over.

Finally he shook his head and got up. "Shit," he said, moving to the other side of the room. "Shit."

"Look, I'm not expecting anything from you. I just—well, it changed something in me. And I never told anyone, I guess because ... because the one person I wanted to tell was you."

Sandy lit the joint. He scratched the back of his blond head. As he started to pace, he had to duck at the eaves, he was so tall and lanky. So he stopped after a couple of turns, and put one foot up on the four-poster. "That must have been—what?—eighteen years ago, maybe?" he said.

"Nineteen."

"And you still remember it. You still fucking hold a grudge against some kid—I was a kid—who used you to get his rocks off one night. Jesus, Elissa." He used her name the way you use the names of people you've just been introduced to, in order to remember them. "Haven't you had anything more important going on in your life?"

"Oh, yeah." She found herself backing away, into the window casement, and she made herself step back out. "Yeah, I have. I got another degree and started a practice, and I married a brilliant sexy guy who became an alcoholic, and I had two beautiful children, and one of them died of leukemia. That's the nutshell version."

"So now, now what? You performed fellatio against your will in college so your kid has leukemia? You got some problems there, Elissa." His voice was getting louder; he'd started to pace again, this time into the short hallway and back.

"I didn't say that, Sandy. I mentioned important things that had gone on in my life, that's all. And some have been good and some have been very very sad. But they don't erase anything!"

"So what the fuck do you want me to do about it?" He'd stopped in the doorway, where he took a long drag on the joint. Grudgingly, out of habit, he held the roach out to her, but she took no step forward. "You come out here, you get me to come on to you, and then you tell me about how I fucked you in the mouth when you were a teenager. What'm I supposed to do, let you fuck *me* in the mouth? I don't get it."

Elissa watched while he looked at the roach, then dropped it, ground the ash under his foot. If she'd planned this ... well, who would? She let the silence gather in the heavy air. Her lungs filled with breath and then let it all out. Finally she looked up, looked him in the eyes. She felt her lips moving, her lips. "I just wanted to know," she said. "If you remembered."

"Well, I don't. I don't remember. For all I know, you dreamed it. Or fantasized it."

"Right." Elissa stepped forward. To get past him, she found herself putting her arm around his thicker waist, like half a hug, and sliding through. "Well," she said when she'd made it safely to the landing, "thanks for showing me the house."

"You're a goddamn bitch, aren't you?"

"No, Sandy, please. I'm not." And she heard the whine in her voice, the leftover appeal to the Sandy whose judgment of a person mattered. Still she stood there.

"All right," he said at last. He held his palms up, quieting multitudes. "All right."

Elissa let herself out, through the makeshift living room and the hanging front door, into the summer air. It smelled of peaches that day, Georgia peaches, as she slid into the hot seat of her car and started the engine. Backing out of the drive, she punched the radio, a loud station coming in from the university. The green trees swirled around her as she shifted into drive. Quickly she checked her watch: three-thirty. Just enough time to pick up Mary Lee.

Bones

For Stephen Tapscott

My dog keeps digging up deer bones. He's too old to chase the deer themselves. He watches them as they lean their long necks down to pick rotting apples from under my tree, and he settles his tapered snout on his forepaws as, leaving, the deer act like acquaintances declining to nod on their way to the golf course. Then he trots out to the woods, to excavate the forest floor after an inferior maxillary or a slightly decayed metatarsus, packed with dirt. He tosses these skeletons around the yard and eventually stows them under the woodpile, where the spiders inhabit them.

I'm bothered by my dog's habit for two reasons. The first is that it reminds me of my own death. It invokes a fear of exhumation, decades hence, in some post-nuclear chaos where the metastasized population is left to grub for roots below the permafrost. My dog is preparing in some way of which I'm incapable. At twelve, he's at least as advanced in his dog-life as I am in my human one, and it bothers me that he feels some need still to think about the future.

The second reason I worry has to do with the present, the immediate. There's been a disappearance in these woods by my house—some five months ago, now, back in the early spring, before anyone thought the ground soft enough to dig in. People say they saw the Dugliss boy, one of those who hang around down by the firehouse, just as the sun was setting, and he never came out. After twenty-four hours they started combing the woods—the trees bare, tracks showed easily in the melting snow—but they never found him. Conclusion was he'd run away, starting through the woods then swinging around by the river and coming out just above Windhaven where he could catch a ride. My neighbors, like Miss Flanagan next door, say he had plenty of reason to run from home, with his father sober one day a month and his mother shoving Jesus at him and his only brother dead just last year. But every time my dog comes out with a long barbell of a bone in his mouth something clutches at me, thinking it's that boy.

I am a bone man, myself. That's what they call me, and the odd thing about medical specialties in this day and age is that even people in a backwoods hamlet like ours forget you were a doctor before you became a specialist. At the general store, for instance, I've heard one fellow telling another about his symptoms. Ringing in the ears, he complains of, sudden fainting spells, swollen veins—clear signals of diabetes. But when the other says, "Hey, here's the doc. Let's ask him," the one comes up with, "No, Charles is a bone man. He don't care about this." They've isolated us the same way they isolate transmission specialists from muffler installers.

It's tempting to swallow the bait. I've done so just once, to my recollection, and that was the day the older Dugliss boy, the brother of the one that's disappeared, fell off the fire truck and I couldn't save him. I found myself denying my profession twice in almost the same breath, like Peter casting odds against the cock's crow.

Most folks hold me blameless. The new group of young people that's infiltrated the hamlet, wanting things simple again, is full of specialists. Tax lawyers and psychology professors, they live picture-perfect lives, in Victorians polished down to the wood, with energy-efficient cars and solar greenhouses. Last year a group of them pooled their resources to lay cobblestones down Old Post Road, the way it used to be. They borrowed the original photos from me—I'm village historian, self-appointed—and wrangled a permit out of Windhaven's board. But all they did was to break up the asphalt and return the road to dust before they ran out of funds. The oldsters blamed me for the mess. Since then, I know, the new people have sent petitions to the county demanding better water and central sewage; they've pressured the state park to restore some of the dilapidated mansions deep in these woods; they've tried to oust the Pepsi machines from the golf course. I'm sure their reclamations will prove beneficial. But I've had no more truck with them.

Miss Flanagan and I sometimes share stories of the old mansions. I see her often in the mornings, when the dog and I take our constitutional through the woods. She'll be standing on the lawn of The Point or the porch of West House, just watching the sun come up, or maybe making a perfunctory effort to clear weeds from the climbing roses.

"I remember," she'll start up when she sees me, "the summer the Astors came to visit. My, but we were important then! That was when they had the train station here, of course, and you should have seen them getting off! Velvet capes, and hats with ostrich feathers, and silk stockings! Their coachmen would meet them at the platform, and call out the names of the houses—y'know, 'West House!' 'Vanderburgh Manor!' just like the names were hotels or something, because no one knew exactly who was staying where. And they'd come up the long drive"—here she'll point at the weedy carriage path we take on our circuit—"and the whole staff would be out on the porch to greet them. I'd be there! In my white pinafore—my, but the starch scratched at my neck. My mum used to get letters from Mrs. Astor after the season, thanking her for the hot tea she always had brought up to the room. Speaking of letters, how's my boy?"

By this she'll mean my son, in New York City. "Fine," I'll say. "He doesn't write much. We talk on the phone."

"That's what they do, isn't it?" Miss Flanagan will say—herself a creature of the telephone, of daytime TV and instant dinners. "The old arts are lost. Why, we used to speak languages! What with German cooks and British butlers and French maids, and me old Irish mum running the show, you'd have thought we were the U.N.!"

Miss Flanagan, bless her, has never married. When Eve and I moved to this hamlet, twenty-five years ago, she "kept company" with the manager of a meat store down in Windhaven. She was untidy about it, standing out on her porch with her blouse untucked, her hair wild and her lipstick smeared, waving to him as he drove south, then coming to our fence and leaning over to say to Eve, if Eve was outside, *"Isn't* he a love!"

After Eve's death, I sank into a black hole. When I finally came up for air, a year or two later, Miss Flanagan's lover was gone, and I lacked the courage to ask about him. She's never mentioned any others. Only when school lets out for summer and teenaged couples cruise Old Post Road or stop at midday in the store, she curls up her lip. "The girls, y'know," she'll say, "were *much* prettier in my day. *We* knew what a boy wanted!"

In Miss Flanagan's day, all these houses in the hamlet were servants' quarters. The gardener lived in mine, which faces not our little street but my driveway, once a private road leading to the mansion grounds. Miss Flanagan lives where she was born, in the housekeeper's lodgings. The town library is housed in the small chapel where they baptized and buried children. The stone church itself was built by the first manor lord, its stained glass brought from a twelfth-century church in Flanders. On Sundays the whole hamlet used to gather there to watch the mansion families fill up the front pews with their finery.

But with all the pretty girls and the languages no one was happy then—that is, they were no happier than we are now. All winter long the mansions were boarded up. The staff was kept on, but with regret, as if servants should have been made to go into cold storage like vegetables. Their children tobogganed down the main mansion lawn on slats of wood. The mansion doctor left each year with the family; when pneumonia or diphtheria struck, one had to send a rider through the snow to Windhaven and hope the town doctor was home that night. Sometimes I wonder: come summer, did people rejoice at having the wealthy families back? Or had they gone sour through the long, empty months?

This summer, new barons have arrived, to take the thrones of the old. In June a short succession of town board meetings down in Windhaven saw permits passed to convert the three houses facing mine and Miss Flanagan's to multiple-dwelling units. Dugliss, the one who'd lost his boys, was the contractor. He walked all three proposals through without a whimper.

I fought, of course. When Eve was alive we'd managed to block a neon sign up on Route 12, a proposal to hire carnies for the Community Fair, and the original plan to put the Pepsi machines on the golf course. It was her shrewdness, her strategizing that did it. After Eve died, the cobblestone group took over, and the first thing they did was to lose the battle against the Pepsi machines.

"We can get them on the septic," one of them called to encourage me when Dugliss and the new barons began to hatch their plans. "You haven't got room for a leach field at the end of your street, and each of those places is set up with a one-family tank. We can threaten the Health Department."

"Nobody knows," I told this well-meaning person—a dermatologist, one of my brethren—"what size those tanks are, or how they leach. They were dug a hundred years ago, without engineering plans or specifications. The board will wait and see if there's a stench."

"We can get them on water. There's not enough pressure for

extra kitchens."

"They'll just promise holding tanks."

"Well okay, Doc, if you want to sit by—"

I did not sit by. I sued Dugliss and the town on behalf of Miss Flanagan as well as myself. I used the zoning ordinance (no space for parking cars, and so forth) and the historic character of the hamlet, which does have a nominal title in the state's register. I hired my son's best friend from high school, now an attorney in Windhaven, to file the papers and make the appearances before the board. And within a few months, I lost.

"My, I'd have loved to see you put them away," said Miss Flanagan. "The waste of it—them coming in here and ruining perfectly decent homes just to turn a dollar. I can remember when that red one was the cooper's, a German fellow. There was a workshop in back where we all used to go and hide in the brandy barrels. They made the stuff themselves, up at the big house—and they always gave the cooper a free cask at the end of the season, to save and get drunk on at New Year's. What a time he had!"

There's no sign of a workshop there now—the red house has been vacant for years, ever since the owner died intestate the winter that Eve and I moved here. The other two had absentee owners for some time, and the people who rented ran various quasi-legal businesses, repairing cars in the front yard one year and selling plaster statuettes the next. One house held a large family whose children seemed always to be standing out in the yard, not moving much, as if they were waiting for someone to come along with a rope to skip.

All in all, three neglected houses. But they're not the only sinners. The state has let some of the mansions themselves go until, between vandalism and weathering, one can begin to see the frame within the clapboard, just like a skeleton when the skin drops away. I don't mind this. It reminds me of my own work. When you heal bones, you're repairing something that lasts. Centuries from now, an archaeologist might examine the multiple fracture I straightened, or the vertebrae I fused. Good work, he might say in surprise. He would see back across the span to my patients and the world they lived in—and to me, the carpenter to their frames.

Still, the real-estate barons were not entering a pristine neighborhood, and it wasn't for the value of the houses that I took a stab at stopping them. Unlike Miss Flanagan, what I feared was not change but regression. We were moving back-wards, it seemed to me, from a village where each could claim his turf to a fiefdom, where these buildings would again house chattel whose labors preserved the life and comfort of an envied few. It was with irony that I listened to her bemoan the realtors and, in the next breath, hark back to the honeyed days when the DuPonts and the Astors visited their grace on the hamlet.

Our suit lost, Dugliss began his work. Each morning the dog and I set out to the orchestra of hammers and Skilsaws, the per-cussion of trucks backing into the narrow driveways. Dugliss stood in the street, usually with a flask in a paper bag, watching his crews. He had been, you could see, a handsome young man, with coal-black hair and strong jaw and cheekbones, his pale skin stretched taut over its substantial frame. But a keen sense of the world's unfairness had touched him early in life. He kept his head tucked between his shoulders, and he glanced around like a dog guarding a kill.

Dugliss has borne a grudge against me since that day he lost his first son, the Fourth of July last year. It happened during a fire alarm. We'd all been sitting on the church lawn, the day winding down with the smell of hot dogs and salt in the air. My own son had been up to visit, the night before and through mid-day, but had left to beat the traffic back to the city. He was tak-ing his girlfriend to the fireworks at Battery Park. He wasn't ready to show her our Roman candles and sparklers here in the hamlet. So I sat in my deck chair at the picnic and watched the little ones tumble around.

When the siren went, a half-dozen men around the grills dropped their plates and headed for the firehouse. You can see the station from the church lawn; but whether the boys had slipped up there before or had torn off behind the men, none of us could later say. We stood up from our chairs to watch the engine go by, as if it were the parade that had gone by that morning. I don't remember where the fire turned out to be. All I remember is standing between Dugliss and Miss Flanagan while that red engine began to accelerate, with three gleeful boys hanging off the back ladder.

"Timmy!" one of the boys' mothers shrieked, and with that admonition the kids looked at each other and decided to jump.

Spitting out my hot dog, I ran to the road where they'd fallen—a place half-laid with the doomed cobblestones, the loose stones kicking out under my feet. The truck hadn't been doing more than fifteen. Two of the boys had rolled and were holding their scraped shins and crying. The third, the Dugliss boy, was sprawled on the road.

I called for a blanket. The boy was lying on his side. I put my finger to his throat to find a pulse, which I didn't. It was clear he'd cracked his head—blood oozed already between the cobblestones—but that wasn't the cause of such sudden stoppage. I shouted for an ambulance, turned the boy onto his back, and tried massaging his heart.

"Hey! Hey! What's the big idea?" said Dugliss, lumbering up to tap roughly on my shoulder, the way drunks do. "Lay off my kid! Hey? Give'm a chance to get up!"

I kept on with my work. I was breathing heavily. "I believe he is doing that child more harm than good," I heard one of the church women say—loudly, I suspect, though at the time it was just a ringing in my ears. I worked that limp little body with CPR until the rescue squad screamed to a halt in front of us.

Then I rode with the paramedics to the hospital, trying electric stimulus along the way.

Someone brought Dugliss along behind. When he learned the news, at the hospital, he went up to me and demanded an explanation.

"It's outside my specialty area," I told him. "But I suspect he had a congenital heart defect. Aortic stenosis, probably arrhythmia. A fall like that can make the heart spasm and stop. There was no way for you to know."

"So what about you! You set his sprain last year, you've seen him around, you're a goddamn *doctor!*"

"It was a freak incident, Ralph," I told him. "Something no one could have foreseen. I'm sorry. But I'm an orthopedist, not a heart specialist."

I tell myself I was tired. I tell myself I had a right to be angry at a man who expected me to see further into things than anyone humanly can.

The real-estate barons did, at least, have to put in a new septic tank for the middle house last month before the Board of Health would grant a Certificate of Occupancy. On my way to the office, I watched with a tiny measure of satisfaction as the bulldozer arrived. Dugliss sat there in the drive—he'd brought a kitchen chair with a ripped pink seat—his bottle on the ground beside him. For a few days they worked; then it rained, and the equipment sat idle while they waited for the ground to dry.

One evening after a sunny day, I came home and let the dog out while I checked the mail. Why he tore over there so fast I can't know. Perhaps it was the week of rain, making him eager and disobedient. Dugliss wasn't in his kitchen chair, but squatting on the back porch steps, watching the bulldozer clean up the enormous hole. My dog is quick and sharp-nosed, so it's no wonder he darted in and grabbed his prize before either Dugliss or the man on the bulldozer saw him.

"My boy!" I heard Dugliss shout. "They've killed my boy! Get back here!"

My dog came tearing down the gravel driveway and across the street to me, a huge bone in his mouth, Dugliss chasing after. He had a shovel in his right hand, and was ready to bring it down on the dog's head when the dog stopped. I grabbed Dugliss at the wrist.

"They've murdered my boy," he said, panting whiskey. "Look what he's got in his mouth, there. My boy never made it to the woods, I tell you. Butchered!"

In my dog's mouth was the largest, longest bone he'd ever dug up. A deer's thigh, I thought at first; then, bending to wrestle it from his mouth, decided a horse's. In the evening light the white surface gleamed underneath the black dirt that clung to it. "This isn't a human bone, Ralph," I told him, letting go his arm.

"What the hell do you know about it! That's my boy buried back there! Come see for yourself!"

"This is the femoral bone of an adult horse," I said. "Your boy's run away."

"That's what you'd like to think, hey? One of them's already dead on account of you, and now you pretend the other's just gone off!" He waved his arm at the bone. "You high and mighty know-it-alls! You think we don't love our family, you think our kids don't matter, but they do! They matter to us!"

I started to flare up. It had been a long day at the office, surgery in the afternoon, and I wasn't in the mood for Dugliss's drunken jibes. He had me mixed up with the cobblestone-layers—and it wasn't their fault, either, that he'd lost his sons.

"All right, Ralph," I said. "Let's take a look."

I shoved the dog into the garage and headed across the street. In the back yard of the empty house, the bulldozer operator and another worker, a young kid I'd seen once for jumper's knee, stood shirtless, staring into the muddy hole. Sticking up from the bottom were the grubby, dislocated knobs of joints, some half-dozen of them, with a couple of smaller limbs snapped by the bulldozer lying on top.

"Years ago," I said, descending slowly into the crevasse, "there was an epidemic of rinderpest in this area. A large number of livestock had to be put down and buried."

"I never heard that before," said Dugliss. "You'll have to prove that, Mister."

"*Doctor,*" I muttered under my breath. Ankle-deep in mud, I pushed up my jacket sleeves and felt around. Whether it was the heat or the effect of Dugliss's crazy notions I don't know, but as I plunged my hand into the muck, I half-expected to feel some ghastly piece of the boy—a knee or a hand, rising up to grip me. Instead I got a clavicle and a torn section of vertebrae, and climbed out of the pit with these.

"Horse," I said to Dugliss, waving the muddy things in his face. "Equine skeleton. Ever seen a human back bend like that? Poor thing had been resting in peace close to a hundred years." I flung the bones down and walked back to my house to wash up.

"Quack!" Dugliss shouted after me. "My boy ain't run, like yours did! He's here! He's under your nose!"

Miss Flanagan had come out by then and just stood by the fence, her apron tied over one shoulder, clucking and tsking, the noise of her TV floating behind her.

During these hot summer nights, sometimes, the kids drive down to the Stop 'n Save and get huge blocks of ice—the kind they used to pick free from the ice house to load up the cooler, before electricity. They take them to the tops of the hills on the golf course. Each of them positioning himself on top of a block, they'll push off and ride down the slick, short grass. As the ice melts the ride goes faster. Sometimes they link legs to waists and made a train.

It ruins the golf course, but I like to watch them at it just the same. Dugliss's son used to ride ice, and my son before him. Miss Flanagan says she never did, but from the look in her eye, you know the others were at it with slabs of ice they'd filched from the manor.

I can hear the boys shouting, now, during these hot August nights. If I go out to the fence, I can see their shadows whipping past the Pepsi machines at the bottom of the hill. There are four machines. They've arrived stealthily, by night, like aliens, and they stand installed like lit obelisks. When it was just the one by the fifth hole, Miss Flanagan suggested we stitch it up a cozy, to make it decent. But with the boys riding by it's comforting to see the glow of the machines watching over them.

"Hey, Doc," Dugliss greets me now on his way to the reno-vated houses. He waves, sheepishly. When his wife's garden bore too many zucchini, he brought over a bushel and left it on my stoop. "Hot enough for you?" he asks when I take the dog out.

But I can't bring myself to return his greeting, or to thank him for the vegetables. There's something hard and bitter, like a sour nut, inside me, and I feel as if it won't go away until that dead boy is found. For I'm certain he's dead, you see—more cer-tain even than Dugliss. I've begun to think my dog, rooting around in the pine needles, is hunting for the body. As if the atomic chaos has hit, not all at once, but little by little, with Dugliss's son the first victim and the local bone man unfit to save him.

So like a guilty party I rebuff Dugliss as he goes about his drinking and his work. He's right: his boy would never leave. As Miss Flanagan, bless her, has never left—as the servants' chil-dren, in spite of the hard winters, never would have left. It is people like me and my son who come and who go; who cause, in a word, all the trouble.

Leaving the Neighborhood

For Mark Couzens

The first thing Eddie noticed when the rain let up was that two mallards had taken up residence. They were swimming around the patch next door where the old fellow grew tomatoes in summer, looking like that pair in the book Eddie had read to too many kindergartners that year. The neighbor's yard was the lowest point on Eddie's street. Long before Eddie moved in, the old guy had told him, a stream used to run where the chain-link fence now cleaved the block; the street itself had been called Great Swamp Way. Every spring his yard flooded, and the kids who lived below and across from Eddie's unit ran over there to squish their toes in the mud.

Eddie loved this neighborhood. When he'd been working a couple of years downtown and had the cash to qualify, this was the block he'd strolled down, evening after evening. He'd listened to Johnny Mathis from next door and to Rachmaninoff from the second floor where the piano teacher lived. He'd stopped in the shadows of maple trees to hear the hard cries of babies resisting sleep. As soon as it came on the market, he'd snatched this place up. Now he babysat the kids downstairs sometimes, or he'd order pizza with Mary, the veterinary assistant. Mary had tried to pick him up when he first moved in; now she confessed all her problems with men to him. In this town full of transients, Eddie was fast becoming one of the settlers. He would grow old with the two- and

38

three-decker houses and be known for his anecdotes, like this one about the ducks.

So long as the yard was completely flooded the mallard pair paddled around happily, all the neighborhood kids running over and tossing them hunks of bread. Neither duck seemed to miss fish in this new pond. They dived for fat worms, and waddled over toward Eddie's building for grander meals. Mary came across from her place. "They're going to nest if you keep feeding them," she warned the kids and Eddie, too, "and the cats'll get the ducklings."

"Right," they all said, one way or another. But they kept feeding them. Who wouldn't feed a duck, Eddie thought, who waddles on out to the street just at the moment you're coming home from work? About time, buddy, was what they seemed to say when they caught sight of Eddie's bike wheeling around the bend. The male tilted his shiny head expectantly; the female paced on her broad yellow feet.

Eddie was near the end of his first year of substitute teaching. He'd gotten certification in high school social studies, but in this market, he would have to move to get a real job. As a substitute, he'd finally made the Preferred List, and drew schools close to home. Tobin Elementary, if he was lucky, or the Fitzgerald school just the other side of the park. Life was a lot sweeter than it had been during the winter, when all his calls came for South Boston or Roxbury, for steel-fenced places three hours away in the early darkness. He used to converse with a recording at six in the morning. He'd press one for "Reject" or two for "Accept" and then listen while the taped nasal voice gave him directions by subway and bus. Several blocks from the last stop he'd enter a dilapidated cement-block building, to stand in for a third-grade teacher who'd gone to visit her sick mother and hadn't left any instructions.

Now Eddie rejected everything on that side of the river. Jane, the Preferred Placement lady, usually called by seven and gave him somewhere he could bike to. Since March he'd been the first person home from work in the neighborhood, and the first to greet the ducks.

"Heyya, Mario," he'd say, or "Look both ways, Luigi." They were obviously male and female—Mario with his jade head and neck, painted plumes flirting from the dun brown of his back, Luigi with her humble feathers, tree-bark color, savvy camouflage. Still, Eddie had named them after the Nintendo figures his third-grade class wouldn't shut up about, the week the ducks landed. His mallards were kind of like video figures—stolid, pushing ahead no matter what strange new obstacles might come their way.

"You guys got any water left?" Eddie asked one day as the three of them trundled down the driveway, him pushing his bike and the two ducks shaking their fat tails and wacking. He locked the bike to the back railing and took a peek. A week ago, pale green grass had started pushing up. Now only a patch of thawed mud, like a big bruise, remained of the false pond. No standing water to speak of. When it rained, the tomato patch could absorb the moisture. The ducks stood by the edge of the yard and lifted their flat beaks toward the sky as if beckoning the stuff downward.

"Eddie, Eddie, let us give them some rice cake!" the kids from downstairs came shouting at him when they got home. They were all in daycare or after-school care, these kids. Their tired parents let them feed the ducks stale bread but wouldn't waste rice cake.

"All right, but you owe me," Eddie said as he broke up the cakes. One kid was scared of the ducks and just tossed crumbs from the top step. Another had gotten Luigi to step onto his bare legs as he slanted them down from the porch stairs. She waddled as far as the bottom of his shorts, and then he rewarded her with the cake. Watching the duck balance on the kid's leg that afternoon, Eddie had the idea to rig up a plank to the plastic wading pool, giving the ducks a spot to swim.

"It's the worst thing you could do to them," Mary said when she came over to investigate.

"Give us a break, Nurse!" said Eddie, full of enthusiasm. "If they're too stupid to figure out that wild ducks don't live in back yards, we might as well help them endure their misery."

"If you'd cut out the rice cakes they'd be gone in forty-eight hours, tops."

"Tell it to the kids," Eddie said, and she did, but they paid her about as much attention as a flea. All that afternoon they sat and watched first Mario, then Luigi carefully scale the board and peer over into the water. Luigi even ducked her bill into it, then pulled out.

"They need a beach, guys," Eddie admitted at last. "They need to be able to run out of the water. Once they're in the pool they're stuck unless they can get up momentum to fly out."

"What's momentum?" said one boy, and his sister, the one on the top step, offered bravely to help the ducks out of the pool. But their parents were calling them—supper—so Eddie emptied the water onto the yard.

That night he grilled a tuna steak on his back balcony and watched the ducks settle onto the newly damp grass. It was a good neighborhood they'd chosen, even if it didn't have what a duck needs to survive. He tipped his chair back against the shingles, caught a note of Rachmaninoff, and tried to feel cheerful.

By that time Eddie had been put in the one-on-one situation. That was what Jane had called it. "At the Kennedy Elementary," she'd said. "Might last till the end of the year."

"One on one what?" Eddie had asked, pouring cereal. "Basketball?"

"It's a problem case. Fourth grader, he bit a kid last week."

"Has he got AIDS?"

"Doesn't say, here."

Eddie pulled milk from the fridge. He was practically guaranteed work until the schools let out. Teachers cashed in unused sick time during the nice weather. Still, it was easier going to bed knowing where you'd be headed in the a.m. "I'll take it," he said.

The kid's name was Victor Romeros. "He lives in the projects on the north side," the guidance counselor at the school explained. She was one of those who dressed in tight clothes, with makeup and heels, so you could tell she wasn't a regular teacher. "His grandmother got custody last year, don't know where the mother went."

"His dad?"

The counselor just looked at him. She had hair dyed the color of buttercups. "The main idea," she said, "is to keep him occupied. He's got A.D.D., and he's hypoglycemic. No sweets. The only thing I'll say for him is he doesn't lie. He does just about everything else, but he hasn't picked up bullshitting yet. For whatever good that does you."

The room they'd found for the one-on-one situation was tucked into a corner of the building, behind the gym. The sun filtered in through two high windows to a narrow scattering of desks. A small color TV had been set up in the corner, and an overweight, coffee-skinned boy was sitting on top of one of the desks, tapping his foot on the chair and watching Tweety Bird.

"Hey, Victor," said Eddie, in the same tone he used on the ducks.

"Fuck you and your mother too, man," said Victor. But it came out sweet, a child's voice.

"My mother's an attractive piece," Eddie said. "Better see the merchandise before you give it away."

The guidance counselor's mouth pulled together in a tight O as she left the room. Eddie felt a quick sinking in his stomach— she was going to report him—but then he dropped his backpack and swung onto a desk. There were only four weeks left to the end of the term. The city needed a babysitter, and no one was hiring social studies teachers for fall. He had little to lose.

"All *right!*" said Victor as the door closed and the next show came on the TV. "It's Morphin Time!"

That was the situation, and Eddie sank into it as into a warm if slightly poisonous bath. He'd been dating a new guy all winter, but it had broken over money pressure. James traveled a lot, on his job, and wanted to come home to good wine and a night on the town. Eddie didn't have the cash and didn't want to be paid for. "Lifestyle choice," was how he'd explained it to Mary. There hadn't been anyone since James. Now Eddie kept Victor amused from eight to two-thirty every day, biked home, and hung out with the mallards until the families downstairs reunited and fired up the grill.

"She's nesting for sure," Mary said late one night, after the others had all gone in and Eddie was sitting cross-legged on the lawn, trying to coax Luigi with salted peanuts.

"Yeah? Where's the nest? What do they use? Old shoelaces, plastic bags?"

"No, I mean her behavior. She's been eating and eating, and now she's real skittish. I mean, look at her."

Luigi had been nosing in after a peanut, then suddenly she flapped away again. Just a week ago, she'd stepped onto Eddie's lap and practically purred. "Well, I'm not doing sentry duty over eggs," he said, not so much to Mary as to the duck. She turned her speckled head sideways and fixed him with her round eyes. "You'll just have to stand up to the felines."

She waddled in, then, and plucked four peanuts from his palm. From the edge of the yard, Mario watched. His feet were deep in mud, a puddle the kids had made with the hose earlier that day. Before going inside, Eddie turned the sprayer on again and gave them both a shower. They stood there in the moonlight, drinking it in.

Victor came in late, and always tired. He watched David Letterman every night, he said, and usually the movie that came after—"unless it's black-and-white, I fucking hate those ones. Nothing ever happens in them."

"So what time'd you hit the hay?" Eddie would ask, but Victor just shook his head with "Fucking late, man," and then tried to stare at the math worksheets his fourth-grade teacher had given Eddie to drill him on.

So Eddie began making them both coffee, Victor's with Sweet 'n Low, and they'd start the day out on the asphalt with a totally imaginary game of baseball. The school wouldn't let Victor hold a bat, but he pretended he was Nomar Garciaparra, and scraped his plump knees twice sliding home. By the end of the hollering and running around, the kid was awake enough to handle the worksheets and even read a chapter from *Our America* before his attention span snapped. It was a good system, except for the time Victor sat at the desk and then slid to the floor, and Eddie found a half-eaten pack of Hostess Twinkies in his book bag. "You're not supposed to eat this stuff," he reminded the kid when they'd finally got Victor onto a cot in the nurse's office, a dank place in the school basement.

"Don't you throw it away," Victor said. "My Granny gave me that." He was staring at the pocked ceiling, his wide child's forehead shiny with sweat.

"Well, somebody ought to talk to your Granny."

"You dissing my Granny?"

"Victor, she's making you sick with that stuff."

"And you smell, man. My Granny is bitchin' cool. You a stinky."

Eddie shook his head. He didn't care. Every day the grandmother swung into the lot fifteen minutes late, in a deep purple Camaro, and she took Victor onto her lap and smothered him with lipstick kisses before they took off. The same day of the sugar attack, Victor had lost it when he was allowed to join his

class for recess. He'd punched a girl in the nose—"She was dissing me. Just like you, Stinky, dissing me"—and the grandmother had come in early and listened, smiling patiently, to the guidance counselor and Eddie. Eddie figured her for about forty-five.
She wore a bright flowered dress, her hair in beaded cornrows.
Beyond the smile, her eyes were tired, more tired than Victor's,
and she kept reaching nervously into her bag for a cigarette,
then replacing the pack as she slipped a look at the No Smoking
sign on the wall. Victor had trouble waking up, she said, and she
had to tempt him out of bed with a little something. He went
to bed late because it was so noisy where they lived. She called
Victor, "my little scamp."

It wasn't for biting that Victor had been given the one-on-
one situation. Eddie had found out the cause even before the
grandmother's visit, one day when he'd gone to the men's room
while Victor did his worksheets, and he came back to find the
kid gone. He had run down to the office and reported a missing
boy, and the playground guard collared Victor at the hole in the
fence, headed for the street. He was going to his fucking
Granny's, he said. *Fucking* was Victor's tic. Twice, Eddie had
offered him a pack of sugarless bubble gum if he could get
through a morning without that word. Twice, Eddie kept the
gum.

"If you'd got to your granny's you'd just have had to turn
around, big guy," Eddie said, outside the office.

"Huh-uh, Stinky. Not after lunch. She just sets me up with
Sega, lets me hang. Three times already, I run there. Then they
put you over me."

"What if she's not home?"

"She's always home!" Victor looked insulted, having to
explain to an idiot like Eddie. "She got a business there, man.
People come in and out. They like me there."

"Come on, Victor, let's get back to the room."

"That room fucking stinks, man. Stinks of you."

"Come on. Finish the worksheets Mrs. Sanchez gave us, we'll have half an hour for one-on-one."

"This *is* one-on-one, Stinky."

"No, I mean basketball. I bet you play b-ball."

"You can't beat me, man. I'm Antoine Walker. I am the nigger with the sweet shot."

"And I ran varsity track. Finish the worksheets."

"You're Chris Dudley, Stinky. You a fucking white boy can't jump."

"Worksheets."

"I'll whip your fucking butt, man."

Later, Eddie asked the office what Victor's grandmother did. She received AFDC, they said—beyond that, they didn't know. A couple of times, as the weeks wore on, he pedaled by the projects, going home. There had been reports of shootings there, as recently as a week before, but except for a patrol car parked by the quick shop across the street, everything seemed quiet. Two tall boys were shooting hoops in the courtyard. From somewhere Eddie could hear reggae. Miles of windows reached up into the metallic sky. He couldn't imagine which one held Victor and his sugar-supplying grandmother. Watching for broken glass, he cut across the back lot and over the tracks, then through the new city park. When he got back to his own neighborhood, he parked the bike and went to lie on the square green back lawn with bread crumbs all over his chest, and let Mario and Luigi come peck at him. He pretended he was the guy from that Greek myth, getting his liver pecked out. He couldn't remember what the guy's sin had been.

When Victor found out, he let Eddie have it, right in the lunchroom. "You're a fucking homo, Stinky," he said in his sweet, light voice when Eddie told him he couldn't have chocolate pudding for dessert. "I don't have to listen to you. You a cocksucker, that's what I know."

Eddie waited until they were sitting down. "What's a cock-sucker, Victor?" he asked.

"You tell me, man. You are one."

"Where'd you get this news?"

"I don't have to tell you, Stinky," Victor said. He dove into his macaroni and cheese. Eddie sat there, figuring. James had picked him up there, at the Kennedy, a couple of times that winter, on bad days—maybe one of the older kids had spotted them. Well, who cared. Victor's broad face had held him in focus for a second, then turned away, as if he'd been making sure to get his target fixed before shooting at it blindfolded. Eddie felt pretty wrecked, that day. He'd been out, the night before, with a couple of the fags he used to know down on Prospect Street, and one of them was dying, so they'd chewed over the suicide option until maybe three. Then, when he'd gotten up that morning, the kids downstairs were all bent out of shape because the ducks were gone.

"And I don't have to do this," Eddie heard himself saying. He signaled the lunch aide to keep an eye on Victor. He lifted himself from the table, his head spinning slightly, to head for the office. He didn't even look back, at the fat kid.

Then, halfway down the hall, Eddie stopped. He leaned against the faux-brick wall and shut his eyes. He could hear a woman shouting, unintelligible desperate words, over the schoolwide P.A. system; he could smell the deep-fried chicken cutlets, the processed cheese. The roar of the children, from the cafeteria, abstracted itself into the dense battle cries of animated cartoon rats. He tried to think of the mallards, the ones who'd left his back yard despite rice cakes and the wading pool. They must have figured it out at last—*wrong place*—and flown off to the pond in Arlington. But when he opened his eyes, his feet were already heading back to the lunchroom.

"Where'd he go?" he asked the aide. She was a short woman with narrow furrows on her forehead.

"Oh—Oh, that one!" she said. She looked up from where she'd been cutting ham for the kindergartners, and put her hand to her mouth. Wildly she looked around. "He was ... he was ..." she said.

"Call the cops," Eddie said. "He's gone for the subway. Tell them to check at Lechmere and Alewife stations. I'm going."

"But—" she said. Her nose twitched.

"Call them!" Eddie headed out of the lunchroom, away from the front of the school where his bike was parked, through the playground to the hole in the fence and the busy street beyond.

It had been a long time since he'd done any running, but he'd taken to wearing cross-trainers in the schools, and his feet pumped under him. The subway was seven blocks away. He dodged an old couple and a group of street musicians outside the Social Security office. No Victor. Weaving across Broadway where cars had slowed for the light, he cut through an air-conditioned office building. A guard shouted, "*Hey!*" The kind of people he remembered working with once—just yesterday, it seemed, or else in another lifetime—swung their briefcases around to stare. Eddie kept running.

As he skipped steps down to the dark tunnel, Eddie fished a token out of his pocket. He passed through the turnstile. Victor was worming his way to the other end of the platform, where the train's red rear lights were receding down the tunnel. The platform wasn't crowded yet, maybe a dozen people waiting. Then two cops, a short older guy and a tall woman, came down the stairs at the other end, neither of them in any big hurry. But Victor spotted them and quickly retreated. He halted only when he saw Eddie.

Eddie was out of breath, leaning a little. "Victor," he said.

Victor looked from the cops to Eddie, and back again. He was closer to the cops, who were advancing, Terminator style. Then Victor ran toward Eddie. Eddie held out his arms. A few feet away Victor suddenly turned, launched past the yellow band at the edge of the platform, and flew out over the tracks.

Eddie dropped his arms to his sides. An idea flashed through his mind: *Let him go.* He felt, in that instant, tremendously at ease. He had given chase; he had tried.

An instant later he'd sprung into a tackle, bringing the boy down vertically against the side of the platform. Victor was hanging almost upside-down, his head near the first rail. Eddie had him by the belt. His own shoulders were slung painfully over the edge of the platform, and Victor's belt cut into his hand, but at least the kid didn't move. Eddie might have been holding a sack of grain, or an iron weight. The train was coming. Eddie could feel the cool air the train pushed ahead of itself, from down in the tunnel.

"Hang tight," called the older cop. He jumped into the trough, hoisted Victor up, and hauled himself out.

Victor's face was deep purple. Eddie kept his hand firm against the back of the boy's thick neck. He told himself he was squeezing just enough to keep Victor from trying anything; he'd learned a long time ago that no one you didn't really care about could really rile you.

"This here jerk," Victor told the vice-principal when they'd brought him back to school, "tried to choke me to death."

Next morning, Eddie called in sick. With Luigi and Mario gone, the back yard felt forlorn. Mary was sure the mallards had found a new nest site, and she was glad. "As soon as I get the right Mario, that's what I'm doing," she'd said that morning. "Nesting. And away from here, too."

"Where the cats won't get your ducklings," Eddie said.

"There you go."

Eddie took the train out to Concord and spent the day hiking around the Great Meadow, watching the ducks and wild geese swoop in and out of the swamp. When he got back, the kids downstairs were building a fort out of appliance boxes, all over the back yard. They peeked at him out of little flaps and giggled; they had forgotten all about the mallards.

Eddie pulled a goofy face for them, then cut away, upstairs. He phoned James, and after a long shower met him down on Prospect, for a drink.

"I thought you weren't going to sub any more," James said after Eddie told him about Victor, about his grandmother, about the subway.

"He's not stupid," Eddie said. "That's the thing. In fact he's probably one of the brightest they've got at that school. You should see him on computer games. And he could probably tell you the name of every guest on Letterman for the past month. He just can't multiply nine by four."

"Weird," said James. He was arranging the tortilla chips on the table, in star shapes.

"He's gotten to me," Eddie said.

"No kidding."

They laced hands, across the table. Slightly drunk, it was all Eddie could do not to bring James's knuckles to his mouth, to taste them. "I'm a starving man," he said. Still they went their separate ways after the drink, though James offered a ride across Harvard Square, which Eddie turned down. Drink always made him maudlin. *Goodbye, goodbye, goodbye,* his steps beat out on the sidewalk. Once he stopped, in the Common, thinking he would cry, but did not, and went on.

By the time he got home, the bathos had passed, and Eddie began to think food would go down all right. He toasted a couple of bagels and sat out on the back balcony to eat them. The moon shone full. Down below, in the parking area, a male mallard was looking up wistfully—Mario himself!

"Hey, buddy," Eddie said, surprised, and dropped him half a bagel, in little pieces. There was no sign of Luigi. Next morning, though, Mario was walking up the downstairs boy's legs.

Eddie tossed him a handful of Rice Chex before hopping on his bike and heading for the Kennedy. There had been another shooting at the projects, he'd heard on the morning news. A boy. Not Victor, but still. And Jane hadn't called, after all, hadn't told him he was being let off the hook, so he might as well bite down on it.

A week went by, and then the last day. Eddie had to admit he couldn't account for Victor. They'd played one-on-one b-ball and a couple of computer games. They'd watched Power Rangers after lunch. Victor had said practically nothing, not even *fucking*. Meanwhile, Eddie was thinking about the next day, and the one after, about the summer and the fall, and whether this whole teaching thing had been a mistake, from the git-go.

And then the grandmother was late. "C'mon, c'mon, c'mon," Eddie kept saying, waiting with heavy, silent Victor while the parking lot emptied. "Just this once, c'mon." She was late, she was always late. Only it got to be four o'clock, and Eddie finally said they ought to give her a call. Victor shrugged, and tagged along while they retraced the long, empty hall toward the office.

When they'd passed the fourth-grade classroom, Victor stopped. "Hey, Eddie," he said.

It was the first time he'd used Eddie's name. "Yeah?"

"Don't, man. J-just fucking d-don't."

"Hey," Eddie said. The hall was so dim, it was hard to make out the look on Victor's face. "What's going on, Victor? You love your grandma."

"She's dead," Victor said.

"What?"

"Dead." Victor's voice sounded higher than it usually did. He was what he was, a nine-year-old, fragile as glass. If Eddie touched him, he would shatter. Eddie didn't touch him. Eddie let him tell how one of his granny's friends had been over, late, after Letterman, and how there'd been a fight while Victor was in the bathroom. How there had come a shot, and then nothing. "I know she dissed him, man, and then he did her. He just did her."

The dull corridor light glinted off Victor's eyes. Eddie crouched down. Victor never lied. "Didn't neighbors hear it? Didn't you go for help?"

"She was dead. I come out of the ... I come out of the bathroom, and she's lying there. Blood, fucking b-b-b-blood all over. She is not coming to get me, man. She is dead."

"Well, but Victor—" Eddie glanced toward the office. No one was coming out the door. "What did you do, after that?" he asked, practically whispering. "After you found her?"

"I went to bed. It was three in the fucking morning."

"You went to *bed?*"

"It was late, Eddie. And he'd gone. And she was dead."

"None of the neighbors came?"

"Huh-uh."

"And then?"

"And then I came here to you. I took the subway."

"Do you ... do you think anyone found her today?" Eddie asked gently, knowing even as Victor shrugged that no one had. The school would have been notified.

Victor was looking at the floor, tears dropping from his cheeks like rain from cupped leaves. Eddie didn't ask more questions. Instead, he heard himself saying, "Well, okay, Victor, c'mon then."

They didn't go far. Just to Maine, with a night on the way in New Hampshire. Eddie had bought a used car that afternoon, for six hundred dollars, and drew two thousand in traveler's checks from his bank account. When they stopped by the neighborhood, to get a few things from his place, he saw Mario for the last time. The mallard was swooping down from the northwest just as Eddie and Victor pulled into the narrow driveway. Mario made a neat landing on the grass. Right away the kids downstairs ran inside to get stale bread. Victor leaned out the car window and watched, but he didn't want to get out. "That thing'll *bite* me," he said.

"Who's the kid?" Mary asked, leaning down from her balcony, calling over.

"Friend," said Eddie. "I'm giving him a lift. Hey, you see Mario?"

"Yeah. I asked at work about it. Luigi must be squatting on a nest somewhere, and he's out foraging. Thank goodness, huh?"

"What a user," Eddie said.

"Hey, they're ducks in a city. Survival of the fittest."

Driving north, his charge asleep across the back seat, Eddie knew he'd bring Victor back before too long, and there would be hell to pay. Someone would find the grandmother, someone who knew Victor lived with her. Eddie would get arrested. He was, after all, homosexual. He had, after all, taken a nine-year-old boy from Boston to Maine. Maybe, by then, he'd have some explanation. The trees, in Maine, rose straight up from the shore, white clouds dancing over their tops. Below, water broke against the rocks, and everything moved.

Rumpelstiltskin

The trouble was he wanted her to give him a child. That was the way he put it. "You can still give me a child," he said. "Brigitte Bardot had her first at forty-four. That's a year older than you, and you've done one already."

He couldn't help the way he slung words; he worked in advertising. He'd just turned thirty-four and was already vice-president of a sleek little firm in Cambridge. Except for a certain nervousness about the mouth, he could be one of those guys they posed in personal investment ads. But when he talked this way, Faye pictured that little gnome, Rumpelstiltskin, and how he'd offered what sounded like a solution: "You can give me your first-born." Which the miller's daughter had grasped at because, really, what choice did she have? And then she'd gone back on her word.

Years ago, for her major in children's literature, Faye had written a paper on how the demands of *trouthe* didn't apply to the miller's daughter, because it was her child we were talking about. In some versions of the story, she'd pointed out, Rumpelstiltskin actually perished for trying to collect his debt. When Faye heard Gerald, now, asking her for her child, he sounded wheedling and sly, like Grimm's gnome, and she could not look at him.

"Giving birth," she said, "is the easy part." That wasn't what she meant, of course. She was in great health; every morning at

54

dawn she rowed for an hour on the river, and the nights when she and Gerald didn't make love she stayed up late reading spy thrillers and listening to Handel. No toddler would ever run her ragged. What she meant was that she had risked enough in life. She had never approved of women who had babies on their own, but she wasn't about to give one to a man, either. He'd lose it, she told herself, the way they did the detergent if you sent them to the laundromat.

Gerald had gone out to L.A. to check on this job. That was what Faye and Gerald called it, "this job," as if they didn't have a name for it yet, though Faye knew Gerald did. It was a copy-writing position, in-house at one of the major production studios. He would have an impressive salary and a team under him, and nothing to hype. If he landed it, and if she followed him out there, they would be married. If if if. If only he didn't want her child.

The morning after he left, Faye sat, muscles tired from her morning row, and sipped vanilla coffee at her front window, plotting as if the child were moving in her already. The phone rang maybe a half-dozen times before she reached for it. Then it took half the conversation for her to realize she wasn't talking to Gerald, and that he wasn't going to ask for what she was holding back. It was her son Hutch calling from the Aquarium gift shop, looking for the shipment of great white sharks.

"I left them under the scuba table," she said. "I called over to Natural History, told them we need that basket they used for the rubber boas. As soon as that comes I want to dump the sharks into it."

"Yeah, well, we open in fifteen minutes. I don't see the box, and Max was just in here asking."

"I'll be over," Faye said.

It was just like Hutch, baldly lying to get her attention. He'd have dragged that heavy box into the storeroom, just so he could call and lay blame. She had to go by Natural History first, anyway, so she got the basket and brought it over. There were three museum shops. Folk Heritage, where Faye had her office, lay tucked away downtown, but the other two sat side by side at the harbor, what Max called high-profile. When Hutch hadn't known what to do after graduation, Faye had put him in at the Aquarium. "I hate fish," he'd said at first. "I always hated those field trips. So dark in there, and all those buggy eyes."

"So join the army," Faye had said, giving him the W-9 to fill out.

By the time they found the shark box—way out back, near the cleaning equipment, where Hutch ventured the maintenance guy had removed it—and set up the display, the place was mobbed and Faye figured she may as well stay. The great white sharks were going fast. They were made of hard vinyl, their surfaces smooth and white, like molded lard. Small boys tucked the missile-like bodies under their arms and torpedoed each other; little girls pinched the open jaws and growled at them.

Max came by, chuckled, checked the register tape. "Neh neh, neh neh, neh neh," he sang ominously in Faye's ear. He ignored Hutch, who thought he sucked eggs.

"This batch is gone," Hutch said as Faye closed up. He lifted the last two out of the basket and charged them at each other. "Whoever wins gets the girl in the bikini."

"We'll need to fetch more from storage," Faye said wearily, "and I've got a morning meeting at Natural History. How about you come by my place for a key—"

"Huh-uh, Mom. I don't keep your hours."

"Well, come by the boathouse, then. It's more on your way, and I'm done rowing at eight. Surely you can drag yourself out by then for overtime."

Hutch had crouched down to reshelve a group of scattered books. "Yah, all right. Man, I'm starved."

"We never got lunch," Faye said, shrugging on her jacket,

"and I could use a drink. Come on."

Uncoiling, Hutch flung an empty book box toward the back room, where it hit the door. "Junior's out of town?" he asked.

"He's looking into this job. I think he'll get it."

"Hooray for Hollywood," said Hutch. "So what'll you do? Manage the Museum of Costume Design Shop? How about the Classic Cinema Annex? No, wait! I know!" He stepped around her and spread his palms to make a picture. He spoke in a hollow voice, like a P.A. system. "Natural History of the Hollywood Hills, Boutique and Souvenir Arcade. Miniature tar-drenched dinosaur skeletons, eight ninety-nine."

Faye smiled. "Not that simple, Hutch."

He checked his watch. "I have a date at six o'clock. But we should talk, anyway."

"Oh, God," said Faye.

From the time he was young, Faye had known Hutch would get hurt a lot, emotionally. There was a certain protective coating he'd never acquired; you could still see the blue veins beneath his milky skin, and the features of his face were always shifting, like clouds. When Hutch was five, Faye moved the family to this city, to a third-floor walkup, their last home with Hutch's father. There had been some trouble with the owner, who lived on the second floor; Faye couldn't remember exactly what. Her husband was always furious with landlords, furious enough to pick fights and lose their lease. A brilliant, unbending fool. One day Hutch got back from school early. Faye heard his voice floating up from the back yard. He was talking to the owner, who was working on his car.

"Hi, Mr. Willis," Faye heard Hutch say. "Hi, Mr. Willis. Will you say hi to me? It's not hard, Mr. Willis. You just have to look up for a second and say, 'Hi.' Like that. Do you want to see my pine cone forest I made in school, Mr. Willis? If you'll say hi I'll give it to you. You can keep it forever. Hi, Mr. Willis. Hi."

Faye had flown down the back stairwell. Just as she got to the outside door she saw the landlord turn as if to swat at Hutch. He caught the edge of the boy's art project, a square of cardboard with pine cones glued on and sprinkled with green glitter. One of the cones fell to the asphalt. Before he even saw her, Hutch began to cry. By the time she had pulled him inside, up the stairs, holding the cone forest in her free hand and murmuring words of supposed comfort, he'd descended to a blubbering hiccup.

"Look," she told him while she eased his book bag off, "Mr. Willis is a mean man who thinks your daddy is a terrible man. Mr. Willis thinks that by hurting you he can hurt your daddy."

But Hutch wasn't interested in how terrible people were. That night, after Faye had given up wrangling with her husband and fallen into a fitful sleep, Hutch's screams woke her. He'd had a nightmare. "I was sitting in poop," he said. "Mr. Willis was yelling at me." Yet the next morning the owner was sweeping the front stairs, and Hutch still murmured, like an incantation, "Hi, Mr. Willis. Hi."

Now Hutch was both gay and HIV-positive. There were no symptoms, though Faye scrutinized him for any sign of weight loss, for the first telltale cough. She suspected one reason he hadn't clicked on a career was that he couldn't see how far his future stretched. Faye knew she had tucked the Aquarium job around him like a blanket because she wanted him close by. His father hadn't a clue. He was gone on a research project for two years to Southeast Asia. News of Hutch's diagnosis would only have angered him.

They walked over to Wharf 29—an after-work bar, a pickup place. The sky was already darkening to cobalt, and gold leaves fluttered down from the linden trees along the cobblestoned walkway. "Fall's here," Faye said, buttoning her jacket.

"How long is Gerald gone?" Hutch asked.

"Three days. They really work you over, out there." Faye caught a leaf as it fell and rubbed it between her thumb and forefinger: top side, smooth; bottom, stubbled and dry. "He'll miss this."

Hutch gave her a sharp look, but without turning his head. "And you won't, Mom?"

"It isn't like I'm basing this on marriage to your dad," Faye said as they stepped inside the bar. "The situation's not at all the same. I mean obviously."

Hutch smiled knowingly, his lips pressed over his teeth. "What, then? You guys have known each other long enough to get over the age thing."

"Two years."

"Plus twelve."

"That—that earlier stuff doesn't count." Faye couldn't look straight at Hutch. They had worked their way into the corner behind the hostess stand, away from the barflies; her back against the wall, she scanned the room for an empty booth. What Hutch meant was that she and Gerald had first had an affair almost fourteen years ago, when she was twenty-nine and Gerald was a junior at the university where she taught freshman comp. He had even been in her class, two years before. She had been nervous and intimidated by the group, and hadn't noticed him. He started hanging around near her office because his advisor was next door. One day he brought an essay he said he'd written for her class, cultural reportage on developing orchid species. *Lyrical*, she'd written on it. She couldn't remember having read it, even with the scrawled comment in front of her and him watching her face.

She was still married then; Hutch was almost nine, crazy about astronauts. He must have met Gerald sometime during that year, at her office or on some innocent-seeming date— lunch or a walk to the boathouse. He couldn't have known. What she remembered mostly about Gerald from that time was

how surprised she had been at his understanding of sex, of what
kind of relationship theirs was—at how easily he separated the
two spheres of learning and love. "I'm not keeping *trouthe*," she
told him once, her hand interlacing his on his unwashed sheets.
"Neither to you nor to my husband."

"What's *trouthe?*"

"Honor, fidelity, truth, duty, straightforwardness. You know,
do the right thing."

"Well, this is my *trouthe*," Gerald said. "You, right here. The
rest," he glanced away from her, as if there were mischievous
virtues lingering in the hallway, "we oughta park at the door."

He had gone away over the summer, and when he came
back she'd left her position. There had been a few phone calls;
but when she left her husband, two years later, she didn't even
try to find him. They had always taken the end of her marriage
as inevitable, there didn't seem any point in the information
that it had finally happened.

"You're sick," she said to Hutch, once they'd got settled
with drinks. "I can tell. Your eyes."

"No, no, Mom. This isn't about that." Hutch poured his
beer into a frosted mug. The corner of his mouth twisted in that
ironic way she'd come to associate with gay humor. When had
he picked that up? "You know my friend Colin, from college?"

"Black guy," she said. "A dancer."

"Yeah, well," he said, "there's no money in that, so he's in
this arts administration program. He says there are jobs. I don't
know."

"Where's the program?"

"Cleveland. Ohio," he added, as if to locate it for her.
"Anyhow, I applied and I'm in. For the spring term."

She heard her own intake of breath, a sucking sound.
"That's sudden," she said. "I didn't know you were interested in
arts administration, Hutch." She ran her hand across the back

of her neck; the room seemed hot.

"Well, sure I am. I ran the box office practically my whole last year of school, remember?"

"I thought that was just because—well, you know. That Joel."

Hutch pressed a finger to his forehead. "I have to do something, Mom. I can't just string paper fish and wait for the cyclone to hit."

"No. Of course you can't." The waitress was there with an order pad. Faye had noticed her before—a stylish, stringy figure whose movements were just a little too efficient for a bar staffed with college-educated would-be actresses. Faye put her at about Gerald's age; she wore no wedding ring. Faye pictured a couple of kids at home, a grandmother left to babysit. The waitress had been lucky to get this job—the tips were so much better—and would be even luckier if the owner didn't replace her with someone younger and clumsier in six months.

Faye ordered a beer, Hutch bourbon and water.

"It's not like you're sticking around here, anyway," she heard Hutch saying. She turned, stared at him. He'd pulled the finger away. Quizzical lines whispered across his high pale forehead; his hair curled back from it, tangled like a thick pile of wood shavings. "I mean, he's going to get that job. Nobody flies you that far for that long if they don't really want you."

"You have a point," said Faye.

Their drinks came. Faye took a long swig of her beer, her throat flattening with the bitterness of it. "But not everything's so obvious as that. He wants—" She'd lowered her eyes until they fixed on Hutch's wide shoulders. Squirming slightly in the new Aquarium T-shirt, he waited for her to finish; he longed to get back to his own plans, his young precarious life.

"I have to give him a baby, to make it work," she blurted out.

"He says that?"

"Not in so many words. But that's the bargain."

She kept her eyes on his shirt—sea blue, with a breeching humpback whale etched in white—and waited for the twin poles of response: *Hey, why not, it'd be great for you* and *Doesn't he realize how old*—? She and Hutch had made it through the worst times together—through days and weeks of sobbing and throwing things around, through the wrong apartments and the wrong schools and wrong jobs and wrong lovers. Yet Hutch told Gerald first, about being gay and being sick. That little fact pointed the way to his sympathies, Faye thought.

Then Hutch laughed. "Jesus, Mom!"

"What's so funny?"

"I must've asked you for a brother for ten years straight! Christ, when Gerald came along I thought you were providing the next best thing! D'you know, after he went off, that first time, he wrote me a couple of letters? He signed them, 'Your bro.'" Hutch gave a little snort and shook his head. "Now he's jockeyed himself into the next generation, he wants to make a new brother from scratch. You remember that time Dad sent me a Nintendo starter set, for my fifteenth birthday? That's how this feels. Like, great but late."

He downed his bourbon. His laughter was good-natured, finding the joke on himself. Faye's throat had gone dry, and she poured more beer. This was how it used to feel, after a long day of work, when Hutch was little and his father did nothing but read books, like they were breaking off pieces of her—the way you might a huge gingerbread man, never dreaming you might eat and eat until there was nothing left. When she found her voice she said, with what passed for humor, "How do you know it wouldn't be a girl?"

"With you, Mom?" Still giggling, Hutch checked his watch. "Not a chance. Boys are your fate," he said, "just like they're mine."

Next day, Gerald's call came at dawn—just as Faye was letting her body stretch over the surface of their big bed, before she got up to go row. "They say they've got one other guy to talk to," he said. "And they say he's a star."

"What's that mean?"

"I think it means I've got the job. Like, he tried to make it sound like a warning, but really he's sick of this process and he doesn't want a star. He wants me."

"I don't blame him," said Faye. "But do you want him?"

"I want you. I want to toss you onto this paisley hotel bedspread, here, and screw the stuffing out of you."

"Mm." Faye slid under the covers. It was a constant surprise, Gerald's desire for her. She had begun to believe in it.

"I want to start," he said, "with your feet. I want to lick between your toes. Fit my chin into your arch."

"Hutch is leaving town," she said.

"Good. We'll all leave. We'll join the vagabonds."

He hadn't said *I know*; but he hadn't sounded surprised, either. He hadn't asked where Hutch was going.

"Did they talk money?" she asked.

"It's a lot of money." His voice receded, as if he was doing something else while on the phone. "I don't mind the money. But you know what else?"

Faye switched on her bedside light and sat up. "What else?"

"It's my chance to call one shot. Not that you haven't been fair. But it's been your house, your town, your kid." He chuckled, the same warm and nervous outburst he used to come up with in her office, in that other life. "I mean, I could never be *Hutch's* father. Let's get real."

He had been younger than Hutch was now. And she would have been willing, then. It would have been an adventure, a blast into the unknown.

"When you get out here," he said before they hung up, "you'll want to have my kid. You just see the glass as half empty now, you can't believe it's half full."

The river was flat and gray as slate in the fall light. Faye
pulled rapidly away from the boathouse. The phone call had set
her back, made it hard to get moving. Already there were other
shells on the water, like giant water bugs dipping their legs
through the film of the surface to scuttle along. From beyond
the thick woods that ran alongside the river you could hear the
rumble of the highway descending into the city. Faye thought of
the waitress from last night, sleeping while her children tiptoed
about her, getting ready for school. Of Gerald, elated, boarding
a jumbo jet in the predawn chill of the West Coast. Such rou-
tines seemed inevitable as breathing, as the earth tipping
toward the sun beyond the next bridge. She bent forward and
heaved back, bent and heaved. Her body was formed of muscle
and fiberglass, and lived on the river.

She passed the third upriver bridge, where the river bent
and narrowed, the current faster except in odd narrow coves
that curled into the banks. Crouching forward, Faye flashed the
oars through the damp air and dipped them cleanly into the
water for the long pull back. Usually she would have turned
around, but today she kept working against the current, her
forearms glowing and her back damp with sweat. The highway
noise was inaudible. Swallows swung low over the water, collecting gnats. As she pulled into one of the coves, sunlight
glanced through the thinning tree branches. Fat golden leaves
littered the bank. In the still water she could see her reflec-
tion—cheeks hollow, neck strained, an unkempt middle-aged
athlete.

She had filled out with Hutch inside her. Her cheeks had
rounded, her upper arms softened. In warm summer evenings
she had lain on her back and let her husband run his palm over
her belly. Then, after Hutch came, her breasts had exploded
with milk for him, and she sat up in the small hours in the

rocker her husband had bought while her son sucked greedily at her. There had been no end to her energy and patience, no doubt that she and this baby would live to nourish each other forever. She could do that again, oh yes she could. Grotesque as she might look to the world, she had the magic in her still.

The shell settled against a protruding branch. Faye flicked a floating leaf through the water, watched it swirl and then drift to a standstill. The miller's daughter did have choices, after all. She, too, lived in a magic world. She could have yielded her child, for one thing. Others had. And the moment she did, she would have found that the sacrifice was a test of her *trouthe*, and the cruel prince who'd made her spin the gold and the gnome who saved her life were one and the same—handsome and also kind—and they would have brought the child up together.

Except ... Faye pushed off the branch and swung the shell around. The sweat was cooling on her neck. Except the child would grow and learn that the miller's daughter had thrown him into a gamble, the way Faye had gambled Hutch. And however many justifications the princess might muster, she would live her life backpedaling, trying to make it up to her child.

Better that the princess had never promised anything, neither gold straw nor a boy child, but had begun by casting her lot against the insatiable prince who would test her and then have her to wife. Not that Gerald was insatiable, or was testing her, unless patience were itself a test. The first night they had made love as complete, free adults, he had stopped, in mid-thrust, and said, "This has got to be different from everything."

"Yes," she had said.

"Or we'll stop. If it's ever a pattern we'll stop. Because you astonish me," he had said, and traced the outline of her breast with one finger.

"Thanks."

"And I want to astonish you. Not ever anything less."

"Yes," she had said, automatically. Though she had thought,

even then, of their ages, and how she would one day come to owe him something. How many people could you owe?

There had been Hutch, yesterday, trying to tell her she had paid her debt to him, and still she disbelieved. She raced her shell down the bright river, with the current, under the bridges, as if trying to retrieve the promises she must have made.

At the landing, Faye hauled her shell out, swung it up onto its rack, and signed herself out. Her eyes blinked in the sudden dimness of the boathouse. There, with the sun behind him in the doorway, stood a slim shadow—Gerald! Quickly Faye brushed her hair away from her face, flashed a smile. But it wasn't Gerald. He was too young a man to be Gerald. He was her son, Hutch, come to borrow the keys to her office.

"Sorry," she said, "I'm running late. I forgot, actually."

"It's okay," he said. Hutch had stepped in, and was looking up at the upturned shells. "You always got up early and did this," he said, "as far back as I remember. And Dad was supposed to feed me breakfast and get me dressed, and I was always slow at it, and he had a short fuse." He turned to her. "I never could figure out why you did that to me."

"I didn't do it to you," Faye said evenly. "I did it for me."

"Well, I never could figure it out."

"Can you now?"

He shrugged, thrust his hands into his pockets. "Hey," he said, "you're in great shape, better shape than me. You'll never be sick. You'll never die."

Her heart swelling as she gave him the keys, Faye watched him go. In the fresh morning he cut a handsome figure—his hair washed and combed, his body not quite finished, ripe for transformation. Nothing like Gerald, who had come to a pinnacle in his life that Hutch might never reach. But just for a moment. And Gerald used to come down there, too, that she might cut short her row and steal an hour in his room. He would take her breath away; and in its place would come *Yes*—not that mechanical assent but a breathing outward, like a flower, until she thought she would never stop the word from blooming in her mouth.

Mud Time

In the first real snow, when you had to put the chains on just to get up Old Post to Route 12, the five miles to Windhaven made a hard distance. Cars fishtailed all over the road. I took the truck, but its battery was low; the headlights showed up the storm just as it rushed over the wipers, and then a semi would come by and kick a load of brown stuff onto the glass.

Windhaven is one of those towns that's spread out along a strip, with a big mall at the far end. I wasn't going as far as the mall, though it might have been better if I had. As it was, I stopped and started the truck three times, spinning in the waxy stuff, four inches by then. My first stop was for children's Tylenol, which April said our six-year-old, Brian, couldn't last the night without. The second was at the supermarket. The lights inside made the place like a carnival. It could have been summertime. It could have been Poughkeepsie, or California, or anywhere.

With their belts hanging from their coats, people swung through the aisles, plucking things off the shelves like they were on a scavenger hunt. I waited twenty minutes in the cash-only express lane behind people who had too many items or wanted to write checks. One bimbo, two carts ahead of me, pulled the trick of forgetting "just one thing" so she could hold up the register to make a last sweep and come back with three—while the rest of us flipped through the *National Enquirer* and *Soap Opera*

Digest and generally wasted our time.

I finally got my hamburger meat, relish, buns, and a head of iceberg, and skidded my way over to the hardware store. We needed a new ball for the toilet, not something that could wait. I didn't see any on the shelf. So there's the customer service line, and I run into Woody Short, who's after a twelve-inch wrench to get his oil tank open since the gauge broke.

"Shopping up here with the swells?" I said to him.

"Well, it's not such a drive." Woody's got these cool, slanty eyes, and he planted them on me.

"Pitiful day for it," I said.

"Yeah, my four-wheel took fifteen minutes to start. Almost gave up and went to Gray's. But then she clicked in."

The clerk came back from the stockroom to tell Woody they were out of the twelve-inch.

"You know who'd have it," I said.

"Sure do." Woody wasn't going to bite. He and Carol have six kids, the youngest retarded. They took the charges against Gray harder than anyone else in the village. "I can get it at that place in the mall. Just a couple miles on."

Of course I could have gotten everything I was after at Gray's too. The meat would have been more but it would have been lean, and he'd have thrown in a lollipop for Brian. Still, I got my tank ball, the cheap kind with the plastic pin, and fish-tailed home.

April brought up those lollipops, I remember, when the thing first hit the papers in December.

"He had a color for each kid," she said, sort of amazed. "Brian's green, Meg's yellow. You know how we tell them not to take candy from strangers? Jesus, why'd we think strangers were the ones after them?"

Some stopped doing business with Gray at the first rumor. April and I, though, we didn't want to judge. We waited—we even let the kids go on down to the store like always, except not after dark—until it hit the papers. Then we cut him off, and I started putting miles on the truck.

The charges were pretty simple. Gray and his wife had had foster kids in their home as long as anyone around here could remember. They'd taken all kinds, too—white, for the most part, but crippled, palsied, stuttering, kids with all sorts of problems that even a natural parent wouldn't ask for. They even adopted one, Samson, who had what they call a "learning disability," another word for retarded. He didn't finish past the eighth grade. You used to see Gray, out on the street on a summer day, his apron tied over his T-shirt, tossing a Frisbee with those kids, and next thing you knew, the rest of the town's youngsters had joined in. A person never thought twice when Gray stopped by the house, said he and a couple of the fosters were going to the ballgame, did Brian want to come along? You'd see his wife, with her little pinched face, wave him away from the big picture window down at the store, then she'd turn back and finish making your ham sandwich or arrange the stick candy. Never an idle second for that woman. You'd wonder how a big man like that picked such a little bird for a mate.

Anyway, the accusation that came down was that Samson had raped one of the girls. Then, with just a nudge, it tumbled out that Gray himself had set the trend. He'd been forcing himself on those little kids for close to twenty years.

A girl it was, who brought the charges—one grown now and working at another mall, south from here about forty miles. Nothing was even wrong with her when Gray took her in, years back. She was just a homely girl with buck teeth and close-set, squinty eyes. Her hair took on the color of city snow. She stayed a long time with Gray, though he never tried to adopt her, and it wasn't until she graduated high school and moved south that she was ever apart from their family.

What she said was that she'd come up for a holiday visit, Thanksgiving, and Samson had taken her out to the RV in back and gagged her while he did it. Next thing you know another girl, a retarded one still off and on between Gray and Social Services, come out and said Samson'd tried once with her, and only because he'd seen his father doing it. Both these girls talked about years of one thing and another, not only with them but with the rest, I think even a boy or two. They said he stroked them and talked to them when they come home from school and the wife was down in the store, and next thing you knew he'd lifted up their skirts. The papers didn't give details— we don't have that kind of press around here. But it took only one read-through to get the whole story. It was then that April put the article down and said, as if it needed saying, "We can't shop there a single time more. I wouldn't let the kids set foot."

Some there were wanting him shut down. "State ought to confiscate his business," April's sister said late that winter. "Spend the money caring for those poor creatures he ruined." She was talking in front of our kids, but I didn't stop her. Seems they knew all about the case in the grade school.

"You can't take away a man's livelihood before you put him on trial, June," I said. "How else is he supposed to pay his lawyers?"

"Same way he's going to pay back those little children," April put in, waving away my pipe smoke the way she did when she was annoyed with me. "By forking over his ill-got buildings and doing his time."

I turned away from them and stared out the window. The snow was melting fast, running mud rivers down the roads to the center of town. We all knew Gray had been picking up property here and there, and now and then selling a piece he'd fixed up to one of the weekenders who seemed to be coloring our village. But Gray was always a simple type, hands like a farmer's, dressed every day in a clean blue shirt, with a down vest for winter when he kept the store cool. It wasn't until this business came out that we realized he'd grown rich as Croesus.

He was even building condos out by Windhaven Lake, those zigzaggy units that sold by the square inch. Other circumstances and no one would've begrudged the man. He'd worked fourteen hours a day, seven days a week, as much of his life as anyone had known him. But now, well, it was like the money took away any doubt that he'd done what those girls said he had—as if making money made you do those things more than being poor did.

Winter moved into spring, and we missed the store. Not so much for the convenience of getting beer and hardware and all that nearby, but more for the easy place it was to be and see everyone. Years back, Gray had got a couple stools and put them by a counter at the window, and any time of day you'd find one or two of your neighbors sitting there with coffee or soup or just a hard roll. You could pick up the paper and go through it with whoever was around. You could take a stool yourself and go through it with Gray. Me, I work odd hours at the main county firehouse, so I always liked to have a place to go to where everything gets back into rhythm. Now and then, after the news got out, I'd see Gray walking his spaniel, or at the barber's in Windhaven, and I had to check myself from going up to him. "Hell," part of me wanted to say to him, man to man, "why'd you have to go for kids? There's women around—more of us find them out than stick home. There's men if you want. This village can take a lot. But *kids.*"

Of course I passed him by without a word. After a while it seemed almost natural to be driving into the mall for our goods. You'd even see someone from the hamlet there and stop to pick over a little news. Soon, you could leave those long walkways feeling almost like you'd been down to Gray's. Some of the talk was about him, naturally, though there wasn't much more hard news to tell. You'd hear how he'd been to his lawyer's office, or his lawyer had come to him, or how some neighbor had seen the girl down where she worked and said she was having her teeth fixed.

April and I were having our own troubles by then, so I didn't tune in much. April was planning to go live at her mother's awhile. She planned to take Brian and Meg along, too, and I wasn't rushing to stop her. The same week she moved out we heard the indictment had come down on Gray. No connection between the two, I just remember the time being linked one to the other.

It was a hard time for me. I'd work at the firehouse and bring home a TV dinner or stop off at McDonald's, depending on the time of day. I hit the bottle more than I should, and I threw money at the numbers. April and I used to start a garden every spring, and now the kids came over on weekends and tried to get me to do it, but the ground looked cold and miserable to me. When I got home nights, I'd wander down to the center of the village and loaf around the empty shops.

We'd heard Gray had closed up the store the day the indictment was issued, which was about the only thing he could do—that, or risk having someone set fire to his stock. Gray's was a terrific old false-front building, tin-stamped ceilings and wide pine floors, but now it had got to be an eyesore. People were saying that when Gray went to jail we should tear down the building and put up a convenience mart, just to start fresh.

But as I say, I didn't tune in much. What I did do was wander. One night, I was standing across the road from Gray's store, my hands in my back pockets, a little drunk, when I looked up and saw him at the second-floor window. The first thing I noticed was the cigarette he pulled away from his mouth. Gray didn't smoke, said he hated to sell those cancer sticks, but cigarettes brought in cash and who was he to tell a person not to kill themself. There he stood with the smoke curled around his face. He couldn't see me, but to me he was like a picture in a frame, a big middle-aged man filling the window, one shoulder up against the sash, one hand at his mouth. He should jump, I found myself thinking, and with my eyes I traced the path his body would take—down the false front of the building, tumbling off the metal awning, then to the asphalt of the road. It didn't look far enough to kill him.

After that night, I came back a lot, to hang around near Gray's store and catch glimpses of him. Once or twice I cupped my eyes to the picture window and saw all the foods and hardware and children's clothes, stacked against the walls and hanging on racks the way they always had. I wondered whether Gray's wife went down there in the daytime and dusted off the shelves. I never stopped to look when it was light, in case someone drove by. At night, though, the place was like a magnet to me; the couple times the kids stayed over, I itched to get out and walk down there.

At first I was sure April'd be back. I didn't have another way to think. April and I had been high school steadies, and then when Meg came along, the year after we graduated, it seemed only natural to fix up a wedding. Plenty of others in the village did the same. And so there was a certain amount of fooling around, because we weren't so sure any of us wanted to be married just yet. Now, I thought we'd settled into it. But for April it seemed every little thing had got to be irritating. She didn't like my pipe anymore. She couldn't stand a hot breakfast anymore. I moved too much when I slept. One of the guys at the firehouse told me it was change of life, but April had years of babies in her. Anyway, I wasn't going to remake myself bottom up, so let her go was what I thought.

One thing I used to notice about Gray's was this: it was a place where men and women both came in. If they stayed to talk, they used words that lay on a common ground, could be picked up by anyone. Things like money and sickness, and changes that kept coming nearer. You didn't often go in there with the one you were married to, but you weren't on the prowl either, so you relaxed. It's not the same at the mall. Malls were made for women, just like diners were made for men. There's nothing can be said in those places that means anything.

Gray used to listen from behind the counter while we stood in his aisles with our milk getting warm or a couple new undershirts tucked under an arm. We thought then he was a philosopher. "Healthy mind in a healthy body," he said to Brian once when we were picking up some spinach and Brian was making faces about it. *Who would ever have thought?* That's what people kept saying, month after month, while we waited for a trial.

So one night I'm down in the center of the village, around three a.m. or so, just off night duty, and looking up I see Gray's room is dark. Now you know he and his wife aren't going out, so I stood there a second, puzzled, when I heard a footstep from up the road. It wasn't until he got within thirty feet of me that I recognized Gray. I was standing there—couldn't exactly pretend I was on my way to anywhere—and he wasn't looking to walk by. He come up and dropped the cigarette he was smoking, and crushed it under his foot.

"Thought you hated the weed," I said to him.

"It's suicide, all right," he said. Gray had a nasal twang to his voice, came of his family's being from Nebraska, though he was raised around here. He was wearing the blue shirt and down-filled vest, like always, only without the apron his legs looked thinner than I'd remembered. I'd thought of them like stone pillars.

"Notice you whiling away time," he went on. "Don't you know we roll up the sidewalk at eight?"

"Restless," I said, trying not to meet his eyes, which wasn't too hard with a cloudy night and no moon. "Got to stretch the legs."

"Looks to me you could stand a shot of whiskey."

"Oh, no. No. I should be getting on home," I said, shuffling sideways now.

"No wife to wait up," he said, stepping back to let me pass. So he knew, like the whole town. Even though he'd made a jail of his apartment and shut the store, word traveled like a smell through the very walls.

"Guess that's a fact," I said.

"So take you a quick shot. I was just going for one myself," he said, and then as if to set the record straight, "I don't bite."

At that he walked away from me, around back of the store, where we all knew he kept his office. I followed. Hell, there's nothing wrong with a man having a drink with another man, not a kid in sight. I watched as he pulled the cord for the light and reached under his desk for the bottle and a pair of clean glasses.

What did we talk about? A little about the firehouse; he'd heard they had a search on for a new chief. A bit about how bad the Knicks had played. Something of a disagreement over how much sports they should show on television. He may have told me that night that Woody Short had cancer of the esophagus. I'm not sure it was then. I know I heard it first from Gray, and it took me aback he'd know before me.

I kept half an eye on the door, afraid I'd be caught down there at the store, drinking with Gray. Once, smashed as I was, I wondered if Gray himself—sitting across from me in his leather chair, thinner than before but his face like always, as if someone'd hewn it out of a slab of limestone—had set it up like this, thinking to rope me in and let someone find us. Anything for a public supporter. But I stayed, anyway, until Gray said the little woman would be worried and he had to toss me out.

I went home through the streets with the smell of the store on me like somebody else's clothes.

Now, that night didn't change my opinion of Gray. Where there's smoke there's fire was the main idea, even though some lawyer wrote in the paper that you could be as innocent of a sex crime as of any crime. "Where, I ask you," said one of the boys at the firehouse, "is the innocence here? I'll tell you. It's in the children, that's where."

I couldn't deny that, but I wasn't in any way for judging. I hated April and I wanted her back, that was most all I could think about. Hated her for going to her mother's, but also for a million other things she'd done over the years. Like picking this house, for one, that was nothing like a place where I'd truly want to live. I banged around in it by myself, up and down its split levels and through its long narrow kitchen. I'd pictured us in one of those farmhouse type houses, with wood everywhere and things I could set to fixing. That was on the list of what irritated April, my always fixing things. But then of course I wanted her back because of who she was, my wife, and also I missed the kids. Sometimes, lying in bed in the early morning, my head a mess from a couple too many bourbons, I'd think about touching Brian or Meg, just their hair or their shoulders, the way you do when they've had a nightmare and you've got to calm them down. I'd think how skinny and smooth they were. And then all at once I'd think of Gray and what he'd done, and I'd shake.

But I wandered again down by way of the store. Again, Gray showed up and we put down a couple. Word traveled. "I understand you're keeping company," April said to me when she dropped the kids off, "with the local child molester."

"Is that what you understand."

"Don't think it bothers *me*. I'll want all the ammunition I can get."

She smiled real broad. April is an attractive woman in a big, good-hearted kind of way. "She'll be as fine at forty-five as she is at eighteen," my mother used to say of her, liking her for that. But now, closing in on thirty, April's features seemed to have gone a little lopsided, as if she were holding them together by force of will. She looked happiest when she was acting mean, and plainest when she was—I think—feeling happy. If she were still going to be my wife, I would've noticed how she was trying hard and would've gone gentle on her. But since she seemed to want to go from me, I only noticed and went hard.

"I didn't know we were planning on a battle," I said.

She shrugged and smiled again, narrower this time.

Somehow I was surprised when they set a trial date. Maybe because it seemed what had happened to Gray already was enough—the store closing down, the whole town not speaking to him or his family, the foster kids taken by the state. All that, put together, was a sentence the man couldn't appeal for his whole life. You had to remind yourself that a jury still lay ahead, and then a jail term, a time being useless that was supposed to pay off Gray's due to the state for what he'd done. When you figured it wasn't the state that had suffered, the thing made even less sense.

Anyway, it was that same time April started the push for custody, and I knew enough to watch myself. I stayed sober at the firehouse, I kept the house clean, and I rolled up the side-walks with everyone else. What I did in my own wall-to-wall carpeted living room, with the drapes closed, was nothing the lawyers needed to tend to. I did more of it than before, being worried about the kids and having to watch myself on the out-side. The afternoon Gray showed up, I had a fifth down past the neck. I heard him knocking, but when I turned my head I saw he had the door already open and was rapping his knuckles on the inside.

"What time of day is it for you?" he said, closing it behind him.

I hadn't seen him in nearly six weeks, and the bend in his big-boned frame startled me. He had the look of a beech tree when the ax first cracks it. You can see the angle it will take when it goes down.

"Night," I answered him. "Always night."

"Shoot, in here it is. You don't get a chink of light through those windows."

"Like it that way. Keeps me in rhythm."

"Mister, you have lost the beat." Gray was in the room now,

and switched on the overhead. "I always wonder," he said, taking a dirty glass from the table and filling it, "when a man stops coming down to the store. I figure something's eating him, so I check it out. Good for business."

"But the store—" I started, but I looked up to find a grin on his face that slowed my blood. "Nice to know when you're missed," I said.

"Oh, sure, sure." Gray nodded energetically. He lowered himself to the edge of the overstuffed chair next to the couch I had myself sprawled in. When he looked over at my lighter, I tossed it to him. "When your wife leaves it must seem like the whole world packed up and went with her."

"Just pussy," I said.

"Aah, not by a long shot," he said, lighting up, while in my fuzzy head I realized pussy wasn't the best subject to bring up with Gray. But he went on, "Now my Emma, she's never been no movie queen. Why we're not even a match—look at us!" He spread his arms wide as if Emma was to be found in them, and I thought of her little sparrow chest being crushed in a hug like that. I chuckled—or giggled, more—with the liquor.

A muscle jerked in Gray's face. "But she's stuck with me through this whole thing. She's not said a word of reproach, and she's not *meant* one either. That's the key. You know when we took in all those kids?"

I nodded and reached for my glass.

"Emma's idea. She saw me pacing the store, up and down the aisles, the shelves all stocked, nothing to fuss over, and she said, 'Gray, you need a hobby. You need to be father to more kids than I can bear you.' That was the start. Wasn't the money from the state we were after, just this—" He looked at the drapes by the front of the house, as if he could find what he meant to say there. "This *window* we could reach out from."

"Gray, no one ever said—"

"You remember Megan Storrs?"

"The little redhead?"

"She said to me once, 'Graysey'—that's what they all called me—'I like you better than God.' I asked her why and she said, 'Because you'll always love me, and you don't make me pray.' She was a skinny, scared little thing when we took her in. Now she's a beautiful woman, off at college."

"No one ever said it was the money, Gray."

"Got a card from her, just today, for my birthday."

"Hey, I didn't know. Congratulations."

His fingers were shaking as he put his cigarette out. "Each one of them," he said in a thin voice, "like a little ray of light."

From my fog, I could sense, even as he lost his grip, how he must have liked to put his big hands around those straight supple waists, those fragile growing bones, the hair on the skin like down. I envied him. And he knew I would. He'd picked me for it.

"So," he said. The bourbon he held soaked up the overhead light, the glass's spots showing. With his head bare, a line seemed to cut straight down the forehead from the crown and carry through with hardly a break to the end of his long nose. He glanced over quick, like he was about to tell a joke and wanted to be sure I was listening. "You think I did it, don't you?"

"Well, sure." The words got out before I thought them, the way they do when you've been alone drinking. I swallowed hard. "Not that it makes any difference to me, Gray. Hell."

There fell a silence. I couldn't look at the man. I wished to hell April'd never gone to her mother's. Blood seemed to pump in my face and nowhere else. *"Didn't you?"*

"You'd like to know." He lifted his glass and downed it, pursing his lips after. Then he clapped the empty glass on the table and stood up.

I was stone sober now, waiting like he was going to tell me that April was coming back.

"You'd like to know," was all he said, again, before he turned and let himself out of the house.

By the time the trial came up in August some young man from the city had opened up a convenience shop next to the gas station up on Route 12 and was selling the things you needed in an emergency. His prices were sky-high and the stuff he carried was all prepackaged by whoever invented these places with their orange neon signs and their serve-yourself coffee. But most of us adjusted. While we couldn't see hanging around by the Plexiglas counter with Woody Short's sixteen-year-old daughter standing behind it like a statue in her uniform orange vest and scarf, we found other ways to pass the news. We got used to ourselves, maybe, being an extension of Windhaven, and not this precious little village we thought ourselves. Cured us of our pride to have to stop at the convenience just like the rest of pitiful America.

When she saw I wasn't coming after her, April didn't move all that quick to get a divorce and custody and the rest. She stayed on at her mother's. Now and then I'd hear she was seen at a place in Windhaven with some guy from the plant down there, but she brought the kids by the house and hung around, too, so it wasn't clear to me that she'd settled anything in her mind. When I broke my collarbone at a five-alarm blaze in June, she took to coming over when she was done work to fix me something to eat and make sure I wasn't doing yard work.

"Stop watching me," she'd say while she was moving around the kitchen, fixing up some supper.

"I'm not," I'd say, though I still had my eyes on her while she turned the meat and unwrapped a package of frozen peas. I stared like I was seeing her for the first time and stopping to consider if this was the woman I wanted to spend my life with. The question had been occurring to me. So many women in the world and here you come down to this one. Thinking about it kept me from drinking, but even with a clear head I couldn't find the answer. Like the snow that melted into rivers or Gray's lust for that buck-toothed girl, my marriage to April seemed a picture I couldn't quite get a fix on.

In the end the jury acquitted Gray on a technicality. I can't recall exactly what, but it had to do with improper testimony and hearsay. Not enough to clear any man's name, especially not Gray's. The girl went off to whatever cynical future girls like that go to, failure sticking in her craw. Gray bought a new RV.

And all that week, following the verdict, the people in the hamlet shuffled around the post office and the main street, restless, like dogs in heat. Most folks just wanted the store open again. Woody Short rasped about how high smokes had got at the Minimart. He was scheduled for surgery by then. He hoped Gray would stay reasonable. On the fifth day, the wreckers came.

"Putting up condos," Gray said when a group of us caught him outside, going over papers with the crew foreman. "Twelve units, six with Jacuzzis. Oughta drive the city folks wild." And he winked at the foreman like they shared some kind of history together.

"Where you going?" I asked him.

"Florida, maybe," he answered, squinting up at the sun. "Or maybe somewhere west. Seen my new sweetheart? Top of the line." He motioned toward the RV parked in the store drive; steel blue, with a wide white wave painted on the side.

I said I'd seen her. The other folks murmured. Gray met them head on, asking if they'd like to take a tour. Some said yes, and scrambled aboard the RV. There was a certain polite amount of oohing before they drifted off, sick with envy.

When I'd got him alone I said, "But you don't have to now, Gray. I mean, you're set. You beat the rap, like they say."

The flat of his hand caught me on my cheekbone and I staggered back a couple of steps. I guess he knew I wouldn't come back at him, though. He fished in his pocket for a handkerchief, which he handed over to me. "Did I?" he said, his voice not even rising.

I put the cloth to my face and got a little line of blood, a wedding-ring scratch on the cheek.

"Well," he said as he turned to go inside, "now at least you know."

The wreckers came, but nothing's gone up on that spot since Gray left town. Some say it's the damn zoning board. Some say it's spite: scorched earth. June claims they never went far, she saw little Emma Gray fluttering around the hospital down by Castleton. But none of us called to check, not even after Woody Short went in there on a respirator.

Late at night, I often walk by the site where the store used to be. April nags at me that I'm like a second-story man, nosing around the hamlet when decent people are asleep. But I'm a fireman, I got to keep odd hours and I have a privilege to act a little odd. I find things in the rubble—drill bits, boxes of rolling papers, stamped tin ceiling squares. I think sometimes I'll track down Gray and buy the property from him, bring the place back.

"With that convenience, now, for competition?" April says to me. "You're full of faith."

I suspect she's wrong. Full of faith is just what I'm not, and what I've got to become. Otherwise it's just when you're ready to grab hold of a thing that it slips through your fingers. I watch my kids, playing outside in the leaves, and it's hard to believe they can stay untarnished until they're grown. But I make myself believe it.

Politics

For Gavin

If her flight back East hadn't been cancelled, they never would have gone out on precincts. They'd have groped each other in Dan's big Ford Explorer in the culvert outside Rolling Hills, they'd have played a couple games of coulda-woulda-shoulda, and Maude would have boarded the one p.m. for New York. Instead, they were begging votes. From house to house they trooped, Maude in her straw hat and blue dress slit up the side, Dan in the cheap silk shirt Sara had bought him in the Virgin Islands. Later, Maude was going to take them both out to dinner, then catch the red-eye.

Meanwhile, Venice. A tough precinct, a hotbed of leftover seventies. Dan had walked it before, over by the high school with its acre of asphalt and broken glass. Now they turned up weedy walkways, rang bells, no one home. Maude wrote the notes, *Sorry we missed you! Don't forget to vote!* with her little circles dotting the i's, and they moved on.

"I didn't know you were interested in politics," Dan said.

"I'm not. I'm interested in what makes you people tick."

"I am not *you people*," said Dan, and he felt what he always felt at some point around Maude, that flash of annoyance and desire.

They rang the next bell. "School Board member Dan Treadwell," Dan introduced himself to the haunted-looking woman who opened the door. "Running for assembly on a simple platform. Safe schools, safe streets."

As with most of these houses, you couldn't see the woman's face. The screen door was made of heavy metal sheeting with tiny holes; she could look out without getting a bullet. Tremulously the woman said, "I haven't made up my mind."

"I'll just slip this literature under the door, then," Dan said kindly, "and you can read it when you have a chance."

"And don't forget to vote!" said Maude as the inner door closed.

If he won, Dan confessed to Maude, he might be able to do something about districting, which had ruined areas like this one in Venice. If he could accomplish something in the assembly, he could start angling for a bench appointment.

He didn't like telling her these ambitions; she curled her wide mouth as if he'd related a mild ironic joke. Back in college, Dan had lived by irony. Adding pounds, he'd shed wit. Now he stood on these porches like an aging wrestler, his butt wide as his hips, his belly lapping over his belt. Sara, his wife, had once been runner-up to Miss California, and still turned heads. But Maude simply hadn't changed. Baby fat on her arms, baby-fine hair the color of straw, the crooked nose she always said she was born with. You'd blink and see her still in the classroom, pale legs folded under her on the hard wooden seat, chewing her Bic.

They rounded eight blocks on foot. "We could finish the list on the other side of the park," Dan said when they climbed back into the Explorer, "or we could drive down to the pier and make out."

"We are finishing the list," she said. She had the sheets loose from the clipboard and was shuffling them.

"Sara's not expecting us back till six."

"Just enough time for the other side of the park."

"Sara is a good woman."

"And beautiful," Maude said. She lifted her hat from her head and shook her hair out—longer, now, unstylish and messy.

He unbuttoned the top of her dress and slipped his hand in. Maude had small, responsive breasts—like the rest of her, unchanged. She stroked his cheek, pulled on his earlobe. "I don't want to be your first infidelity," she said.

As he started the car, a young boy ran down the sidewalk, Dan's leaflets waving in his hand, and rapped on the car door. Dan buzzed down the window. "My mom says," the boy reported, out of breath, "she doesn't want these things. She says they're fastest."

"Fascist," corrected Dan. "And your mom is wrong."

As he tucked the pamphlets back into the zippered bag, he glanced over at Maude. She had her head against the door frame and was looking bemused at him. "I probably shouldn't have helped," she said.

"I'm the best man for the job!"

"So was Richard Nixon."

"Give me your mouth," he said.

She leaned over, smelling of lilac and the salt air. But Dan, in his lumpy body, with his politics like bad-fitting clothes, could feel the solid part of her pulling away.

They found Sara contemplating the wall of the living room. Beside her, photos of Maude's kids lay atop antismoking pamphlets and decorating brochures. "Too much yellow," Sara said.

"No kidding," said Dan. "It'll hurt my eyes in the morning."

"Frannie's mixing me up some ochre. I'll stipple the last coat."

"Stipple," said Maude. "Is that what gives it that sort of scratchy effect?"

"It's a technique," said Sara. She shifted on the couch. She had worked hard on this living room, whose walls when they moved in had been flat ivory, like the rest of the condo. Maude would never have thought to change them. "How was the precinct?"

Sara had recently cut her hair, and Dan couldn't quite get used to seeing so much of her neck. The mole on the side, just below what you could now see was her hairline, stood out like an inkblot on blank canvas.

"The Venice people liked Dan," Maude was saying.

"Not all of them," Dan said. He reached for three glasses, Scotch for him, Merlot for the girls. The sight of the red wine brought saliva into his mouth, and he swallowed. "We were a little to the right of some of their positions."

"Don't tell me you started debating!"

"Not really. Just handed out the flyer, you know."

"They called him a fascist," Maude said. Her eyes slid over to Dan's.

"Fastest," he corrected.

"People in Venice." Clucking her tongue, Sara rose from her chair. She walked like someone carrying a baby, or a book on her head. "Dan should have stuck with the school board," she went on. "He had all these great ideas. About bilingual education, you know, and remedial ed."

"Make 'em all wear dunce caps, I say," said Dan. "Rap their knuckles with the ruler."

Maude was still studying the stippling effect. "What about condoms?" she asked.

"Make 'em wear condoms," said Dan. "On their noses, when they pick their snots in class."

Sara shook food out for the cats, who came pattering from behind the sheeted sofa. Through the French doors, the lowering sun turned the yellow walls a sickening color. "I'm going up to the roof," said Dan. "Want to come?"

Maude looked to Sara. A polite girl, Maude. "Not me," said Sara.

Cool, on the roof. Theirs was the highest, the other condos descending the slope westward. Always a breeze. When he first took the place he'd had plans. Put in a railing, an oak deck, margaritas on the roof. But condo regulations discouraged, and Sara would never come up. A lonely place, Dan and the sunset, Catalina at the horizon. Like that guy in *Catch-22*, up in his tree.

Only now Maude. Her head peeked over the roof edge, her transparent face. You could see the bones in Maude's face. "Hey cutie," Dan said. He grinned. The Scotch working its way.

"This your veranda?"

"Penthouse garden," he said. He gestured at the bleached gravel, the tar.

"Can't knock the view. Sara?"

He shook his head. "She gets dizzy," he said.

"What is it with you and her, anyway?"

"What d'you mean, what is it?"

"Danny boy," she said. She touched the top of his shoe with her sandaled foot. "I've known my share of married guys messing around. But you." She'd brought her wine, and sipped. "I thought you were trying to have kids," she said.

"We were."

"And?"

"Sara can't."

Maude raised her eyebrows skeptically. "That what the experts say?"

"Decidedly."

"That's a shame. I've always thought of you as a dad. I mean, not as *my* dad." She went up on tiptoe, pulled down the back of his silk collar, nipped the nape of his neck. He circled her waist. She fit nicely under his arm. Sara, being taller, had to duck her shoulder under his.

"I used to, as well," he said. "And not your dad."

"There's other ways. There's adoption."

"Please, Maude. Please."

The sun was at the horizon now, a flat orange disk. Dan finished his Scotch. From below he heard Sara, calling them.

Maude wasn't quitting. "You would want white, though, wouldn't you?" she said.

"That's not the point," said Dan.

"Well, then, I'm not sure what the point is."

"Lies."

Maude turned to face him, her head in silhouette, tipped rightward. "I give up."

He set his glass on the gravel. "Sara knew," he said, not looking at Maude, "that she couldn't have children. She'd been married before. Just briefly, but she'd been checked out. In vitro, the whole bit. But she didn't tell me until we'd made appointments, gotten tests." He rubbed Maude's upper arms as if they were cold, which they were not. "That's what I can't take. That she hid a thing like infertility from me. As if—"

Maude was smoothing the front of his shirt. He could smell her perfume, something dusky and sweet, like moonvine. "As if you'd forgive and forget?" she tried.

"Love," he said. "Sara thought because she loved me so much, whatever was blocking her from getting pregnant would just go away."

"And when did you find out the real scoop?"

"Two years ago. Since then"—Dan drew in his breath and let it out, *plead your case, Counselor*—"we've had sex maybe a half-dozen times."

"You or her?"

"She doesn't see the point in it. Maybe I don't, either."

"Poor Dan," Maude said. It wasn't pity in her voice, but it wasn't exactly irony, either. She said *poor Dan* the way you'd express sentiment about a population wiped out in a foolish, distant war.

In O'Donnell's Fish Palace, Maude sat across from Sara. She heard about the antismoking legislation that Sara was so proud of getting through the county legislature. Heard the statistics, the latest findings. The poster campaign, the TV spots. Sara, an evangelist for the cause.

"It's a big challenge, your work," Maude said.

Dan ordered a second Scotch. Magnificent Maude. Maude whom he'd missed by a hair. Maude the politician. She leaned her soft shoulder in Dan's direction; that slight curl to her mouth. And yes, he was sick of Sara's antismoking shtick, it was simplistic and righteous and cornball. He knocked back his drink and started to signal, but kept his hand down. Instead his leg crept out, under the table, rubbed against Maude's.

He liked O'Donnell's. And had to admit that going out into the evening, walking the streets of Redondo as the salt breeze cooled, gave a lift to his days. Coming in here, people had stepped up to shake his hand. They smiled at his beautiful wife. The polls allowed him an edge. If a gaping hole had been torn through his life, if he heard the wind howling through that hole, he was still a man to be envied. And now here was Maude, using up her per diem on him.

"If Dan gets elected," Sara was saying, "we'll get a grant to go into the prisons. You know that the rate of lung cancer among convicts is more than twice the normal population?"

"Sara wants our jailed crack dealers to live long and healthy lives," explained Dan. The waitress, a blond Amazon with a navel ring, slid an appetizer plate of soft-shell crab onto the table, and he tore at one pink leg.

"You can see, Maude," said Sara, taking part of a crab for herself and squeezing lemon over the rest, "why my husband and I have a lively marriage."

"I never doubted that marriage to Dan would be lively," said Maude.

Half a crab remained. He forked it. Yes, he was lively. Always he had been lively. "I could do with some earnestness in my life," he'd said to one old friend, at the wedding, and the friend had laughed and said, "They call it earnestness, now?"

After the crab came soups and fluffy rolls. "A light repast," Dan said. He glanced self-consciously at his middle-aged belly—and then, as Maude deftly took the check, at his watch.

"I'm fine," said Maude. "I've just got a carry-on."

"I believe," said Dan, "in getting to the gate in plenty of time."

"I don't." Maude signed her name on the Visa slip, an elaborate M. "I hate airports. The plane never leaves *ahead* of time, does it? And they can't give away your seat till ten minutes before departure."

"But traffic," said Sara.

In the crowded restaurant, baskets of fresh rolls passing over his head, ginger chicken at the next table, Dan smelled again the scent of her, from the moment in the Explorer when he'd plunged his hand down there—and she had moved, yes, she had risen to meet him, and then when he'd made himself stop he'd put his own fingers to his mouth, and tasted her. There was no reason he should be smelling her now, it was just a trick of the body.

"You remember that camping trip?" he asked suddenly. "To Baja?"

"What trip?" said Sara.

"No, I meant Maude."

"You mean last year of college, when we all went skinny-dipping?"

"Yeah," he said. He picked at the netting on the votive candle. The women stared, what was his point? "Didn't we eat soft-shell down there?" he asked.

"I don't think so," said Maude. "That was in September. Out of season."

"My mistake," he said. How white Maude's skin had been against the blue water, a bone on the waves.

"What's Baja got to do with her making the plane?" Sara asked.

"I know," said Maude.

"You do?" God, thought Dan—the image of her, naked on the waves, traveling to his cock—she is brilliant.

"Sure. We were late, everywhere we traveled on that trip. Six of us in the car, and five of us didn't care. But Dan here stayed on schedule. Right, Counselor?"

It was Sara's hand that slipped over his thigh. He rose. "If we're early at the airport, Maude," he said, "I'll buy you a drink. Deal?"

"You should buy us both drinks," Maude said. She touched Sara on the shoulder, like a sister.

"Oh, I'm tired," said Sara. "Dan'll drop me off home, I'm going to bed."

She was, too. Dan could see Sara's meds at work, in her eyes and in the way her shoulders slumped a little as she stood up. But Maude looked alert, like a deer sniffing the air. This was not a set-up, he would have to tell her. Not that she would care, by then.

Back on Pacific Coast Highway, headed north again like some continuous-loop video, Dan messed with tapes. Popped one in after another—Steely Dan, Dave Mathews, nothing fit the moment. Maude's fingers loosed a button on his shirt.

"That is such a turn-on," he said. The new Dylan in the deck now.

"Touching your nipple, you mean?"

"Yeah. Yes."

"Don't crash the car."

"I never crash a new car."

"Should I stop?"

"No."

He swallowed, mouth dry. They passed a Treadwell billboard, gleaming red and blue in the slanting light. Where the wife and kids belonged, in the protective lean-to of Dan's blue-jacketed arm, they had placed a pair of poster kids from the

Redondo second grade. They had thought of posing just Sara, but the ad guys said it wouldn't play as well.

"Are you going to win?" Maude asked. She had his left nipple pinched between her thumb and forefinger.

"I've got a chance," Dan said. He took a left at the light, where the signs for the airport pointed right.

"And then?"

"And then maybe we'll adopt. Or find a surrogate mother."

"Yech."

"I wasn't asking you to do it."

He drove away from Sepulveda, out toward the beach. Maude's right hand slipped from his nipple, but her left stayed on his shoulder. At the dunes he took a right. No lights out this way, only the white foam of the breakers under the moon. If her flight hadn't been cancelled, that morning, he'd never have thought of this. Fate and the airlines, working together. Up ahead, he spotted a wide turnout in the shoulder. He put on his blinker; pulled the car over. Eight fifty-five, the green clock read.

"I can understand," Maude said quietly, "why she lied to you."

"Can you?" Switching off the ignition, Dan leaned his head back on the seat. They were at the back of the airstrip; planes took off over their heads, but no one passed them on the road. His hands went to Maude's body idly, like part of the conversation.

"There are new technologies," he said. "I didn't tell you. She's participating in a research project. Womb nesting. The women take certain drugs."

"How much hope do you have for that?"

"Zilch," said Dan.

Maude leaned over and kissed him, her mouth honey in the salt air. "How awful for you," she said.

And though he didn't really believe she thought it awful—there was, after all, the solidarity of women to reckon with—he began kissing her for real now, his tongue pushing into her mouth. Gently he pushed her legs apart and put his hand between them. "Maude," he said. He tried to swallow, couldn't. "Dirt Road Blues," Dylan wailed. "I really want to fuck you," he managed to say.

Maude drew away from him toward the window, craned her neck to look at the lights on the aircraft bellies. "Nah," she said.

"But I thought you—" Saliva got in his way again, thick at the back of his mouth.

She turned toward him. She was grinning, her white teeth in the moonlight. She took his fingers with the tips of hers. "We were teasing," she said. "Flirting. I mean, c'mon, Dan. We *have* fucked."

"Twenty years ago."

"You mean it doesn't last?"

"Maude. C'mon." He hitched over on the seat; he leaned into her face. "I could make you," he said. "I could seduce you."

"You could take me to the airport, is what you could do."

He held her chin in his hand. He remembered a time, long back, when he'd taken Maude to bed after a beach party. Inexperienced, she had seemed, and needy. Sweet in the sack, but too unconventional to make a girlfriend. Even then he'd considered himself a politician. He took the long view, he made sound choices.

"Move to California," he said.

Maude squeezed his hand once and pulled hers away. Moonlight outlined the crooked profile of her nose. He pictured doing her in the back seat, the curve of her belly, buck and heave. His cock was iron. He started the engine, spun the car around.

At home, he parked the Explorer in its assigned space below the condo and crept up the carpeted stairs. The light was on in the bedroom, but Sara wasn't there, nor was she crouched over paint catalogs in the living room. He mixed himself a drink and wondered. Then he heard the scrape of gravel, over his head.

She was crouching not far from the edge of the roof, her nightgown blowing around her ankles. "I got dizzy," she said, "so I lowered my gravity."

"That's smart," said Dan.

"I think it's those meds, that make me dizzy."

"You don't have to take them," said Dan.

Sara stood up and turned away from the roof edge. "She's gone, huh?"

"Yup. Had a drink, caught the plane." He pulled off his jacket and settled it around her shoulders, her cold neck.

"You fuck her?"

"No."

She gave a quick little nod, as if he was confirming something she'd known. "I don't want to see her here again," she said.

"I don't think that's so likely."

"Not ever."

"Okay, Sara."

"Meet her somewhere else. Bang her till she drops."

"Sara, cut it out. We didn't even go that far."

"Don't run for office with me, Dan. You have no idea how far people go."

He kissed her then, on her bare neck. The nerves in his lips and skin felt exploded, amok. "Come on down," he said.

"In a minute." When he looked at her curiously she added, "Make us some herb tea. You've got that Lions meeting in the morning, you don't want to go baggy-eyed."

He descended the ladder, passed through the mustardy living room. There on the side table they lay, the photos of Maude's family. He had not picked them up. It was Sara who had sat with Maude, pointed to the gray husband, the giggling kids. It was Sara who had said the politic thing, *How you must love them.*

Husband Material

In the restroom of a tiny hangar outside Peculiar, Missouri, just north of the Ozark Mountains, a poker-faced young woman crouches over a porcelain mug. On its side grimaces a caricature of John Lennon; a metal coil is immersed in the water. Above Tina's bowed head, the restroom fan whirls and clinks, as if a paper clip is stuck on one of the blades. Under her nose, the floor tiles are arranged in interlocking L's, black hooking white. Anyone coming in right now—the door lock is broken—would think Tina to be praying or vomiting, or perhaps looking for a contact lens. But she is waiting on her brew.

Tina's mother's husband has flown her from Little Rock to Peculiar in his new four-seater plane, for amusement and to show off his piloting skills. They've been having drinks in the hangar's rickety bar—two double martinis for Marvin, a Lite beer for Tina. She shouldn't even have the beer—you're not supposed to have anything in your stomach—but she's stayed away from the pretzels, and the alcohol's gone through her digestive tract relatively fast.

It tastes like hot mud. Tina's friend, Ashley, has told her she can't cut it with honey or anything; her stomach has to take it completely straight. "I gave it to my friend Renée and it worked in like her fifth month," Ashley said a week ago, back in New York. "She almost bled to death, but it worked." But that's Ashley, always talking about her friends, as if she's lived a

96

hundred different lives and each one of them a separate world.

Lucky thing there's a working outlet in this restroom. PECU-LIAR MO, the sign outside had announced, WHERE PEOPLE 'R PLEASED WITH YOU. Muzak filters in from the hangar lounge: "How Can People Be So Heartless?" from that old Sixties musi-cal, arranged for violins and a snare drum. Tina smiles at the irony. In the cracked mug the water boils—fog at first, then small air bubbles, then surface motion. From her bag Tina draws out two caplets full of what looks like curry mix—that's the goldenseal—and plunks them in, followed by a teaspoon of brown powder from a sealed Baggie. Blowing on the surface of the water, she starts to sip.

"You okay in there?" Marvin calls a minute later from out-side the door. His voice is a little slurry. There's been just the two of them in the hangar bar—no chance, in fact, of another woman needing this toilet.

"Fine!" she calls back. "Be right out!"

Quickly, Tina gulps the rest of the tea. It burns the roof of her mouth, but somehow it tastes less foul when it's hot. She sprays Binaca on her tongue. Wiping the mug clean, she stash-es it along with the still-warm immerser in her handbag. Ceremonially flushing the toilet, she unlocks the door and emerges into the harsh light of the bar. Marv's ordered another drink, but she doesn't sit down at the table.

"Is my peculiar crew ready to head back?" he asks, looking up at her through his thick bifocals.

"At your command, Pilot," says Tina. She starts to take a pretzel on the way out, then drops it and puts her finger to her tongue, to taste the salt.

It was just a week ago that Tina found herself slogging through the slush of West Nineteenth Street to get to that place. So dark it was, tucked into a wasteland of fabric ware-houses and wholesale furriers, past trucks wedged in the ice between half-open garage doors and the muck of the street, that she blinked and stared for a few minutes after the door had tinkled behind her. Warlock Wisdom, the sign read above the counter. She untied the belt of her raincoat and shook off the ice crystals before they got a chance to melt. Those silly boots she'd worn—ankle-length high heels with one of the heels threatening to come off each time the slush sucked at it—froze her feet as she made out, across the back of the cash register, a logo of two entwined snakes supporting a skull, with waves of what appeared to be light emanating from it.

"Peace," a voice said, mockingly, and Tina saw the guy sitting behind the counter, a white guy with dreadlocks past his shoulders and a face like the skull on the logo.

"I called," Tina said.

"Yah, the herbs." He shuffled his feet on the rung of his stool, but didn't get up. "In the back," he said.

"Right." Tina headed back that way. A lone fluorescent tube flickered just below the high, narrow ceiling. In the middle of the aisle stood a revolving case, the kind meant for paperback books, stocked here with white labeled packets and eyedropper bottles of amber liquid. She spun the thing, slowly. Everything was alphabetized. Tina checked the list Ashley had given her. Goldenseal. Squaw vine. Mugwort, pennyroyal, valerian root. Warlock Wisdom had everything, only the goldenseal came bulk, not in capsules. Dissolve two capsules, Ashley's recipe said, and Tina didn't know how much that was. "I need capsules," she said to the guy, when she brought it all up to the counter.

He looked at her funny—You're gonna melt it all together anyway, why pack it in capsules?—but got a jar down from the shelf behind him and counted out thirty clear caps. "These oughta be enough," he said.

She mixed the first cup in her New York apartment, after writing short epistles in her diary to two former lovers and her mom, in case the herbs killed her. The second cup was on the jetliner, heading back here to Arkansas. She asked the flight attendant for hot water and a tea bag which she tucked into her purse. The guy sitting next to her glanced over once, at the smell, but turned politely back to his thriller. From her window seat she reviewed the landscape below, lifeless plains and low hills with patches of tired snow.

"Your mom," Marv is saying now, opening the passenger door to his prop for her to climb in, "refuses to go up anymore with me. Says she's lived out eight of her lives already, can't spare the ninth."

"How are you two getting along?" Tina asks, strapping herself. It always amuses her to hear about something of which her mother, Elaine, is more frightened than she is. Elaine doesn't scare easy.

Marvin blows air into his cheeks, then lets it out in a whistle. It's only when he's not joking that you can see how homely he is—his thick glasses hiding watery eyes, his cheeks sagging over his jawline. "She is a cat," he says finally.

"There are some who could've warned you."

"My business is in trouble," he says. After punching a couple of buttons on the control panel, he takes off his bifocals and polishes them with his shirttail. The engine is rumbling low. Slowly, the propeller to Tina's right starts to turn. "Tax problem. We are getting our ass reamed out right now by the government. We may go into Chapter Eleven."

"You're not telling her that, though, are you?"

Marvin smiles, one side of his mouth twisting the way it does when he finishes a dirty limerick. "You think I'm going to make this any easier for her?" he says, and ups the throttle.

Husband material, Tina's mother called Marvin before they married. "Hefty in the body, hefty in the bank," she said. Well, she bet right on the body part. For the rest, better luck next time. It is hard to spot good husband material. All in all, Tina's mother has not done too badly. Tina, on the other hand, can't seem to recognize the stuff at all. The last time she visited Little Rock, she went with her mom to a fundraiser for the Zoo Association. "Look sharp," Elaine had advised her. "This group is crawling with husband material." But Tina couldn't see anyone she could imagine sleeping with, much less waking up to.

"There once was a caveman named Dave, who kept a corpse in his cave. He said with a grunt, 'It's mighty cold cunt, but think of the money you save!'" Marvin's rubbery face stretches into a clownish grin as they lift over the trees.

Tina tries to laugh, but she's left her stomach behind on the tarmac, and it's too big a challenge. Elaine would manage to laugh. She still laughs, every time, at Marvin's jokes, finishing the moment with a shake of her silver head and *Oh, you are so bad.*

Last night there were hillbilly jokes, Episcopal-bishop jokes, lewd limericks. Tina, now gripping the sides of her seat in the plane, can't remember a single one of them. Only the filet mignon her mother served, and how she had been ready to eat, an hour after drinking down her poison, but her stomach flipped at the sight of the strawberry-pink meat.

"Betcha don't get meat like this in New York," was what Marvin had said, slicing into his. "How much you bringing down these days?"

"Twenty-one," Tina said.

Elaine set down her fork to cry her outrage. "Slave wages," she said. "Why, your brother Brent makes twice that right here in Little Rock, and he's just a year out of college!"

"It's the recording industry, Mom. Doesn't pay."

"Fuck 'em," said Marvin. "Tell 'em you want another ten a year or you're outta there. They'll sit up. I guarantee."

Tina tried to chew a bite of the meat, which tasted like chalk.

"Or come back here," said her mother. She'd stopped eating

and lit a cigarette. Later, she would gobble scraps in the kitchen, like a maid. "Take a breather, look around."

She didn't say, "look around for husband material," but Tina knew what she meant.

"Now there's the idea," said Marvin, winking broadly at Tina. But Elaine only sighed and blew smoke. At fifty-eight, a uniquely beautiful woman—chiseled bones, softly curling hair, a silver fox.

All her life, Tina thinks as the plane climbs, her mother has trailed men behind her, like dust motes in light. Whereas Tina doesn't know how to recognize husband material, much less purchase it. And here she is home, sneaking poisonous herbs like a teenager sneaking smokes.

Below the plane, the Ozarks bristle with bare trees. It's not the best time for a visit to Arkansas. Deep in her throat, Tina tastes squaw vine and goldenseal. The plane climbs.

"Your mom is the best, though!" Marvin's shouting over the engine roar. "And don't you forget it!"

"I'm not arguing with you, Marv!"

"You don't take after her!" he says, glancing Tina's way. With the headphones over his ears, he looks like a fat bug. "Don't be insulted!"

"I'm not!" she says.

As the plane levels off, Marvin starts singing French cabaret songs. The four-seater rocks and trembles. Tina keeps wanting to ask how he learned French. She knows he fought in Korea, but they don't speak French there. *"Jeanneton prend sa faucille, la rirette, la rirette,"* he sings. It's a bawdy song about a girl and four men. Watching the hills below them heave upward, Tina thinks of her mother's face, so often tipped up, listening to a man. Whenever she stands next to Elaine, Tina feels ungainly. Her own features are broad, the eyes set wide apart. More than once a man has said he could drown in her eyes, but she doesn't count this an advantage.

The flight is taking too long. The chatter from the radio has turned to static. Around them, dark clouds gather. Marvin's not flying straight, not paying attention to how the needles jump and spin on his control panel. "Marv!" Tina shouts across the space between them. "Are we all right?"

"Bit of turbulence," he shouts back, and pulls on the stick so they start to climb. She can't make out his face. Her stomach is enacting its own tornado, the vertigo sucking in all her energy, even the energy to worry about staying alive in this plane with her mother's drunken husband. They climb and climb, above the mounted clouds, the hilly view of the land. The engine labors. Marvin's onto the cabaret songs again.

Then something happens. At once, the engine is silent. The nose of the plane is pointed at the blue sky, like a dog sniffing the wind. The silence slaps at Tina's ears. "What's wrong," she thinks she says, but she can't be sure any sound actually comes out.

"Stall," Marv says. He's flicking switches, staring straight ahead. They hang there, while he works the panel. One of those cartoon characters, like Wile E. Coyote, comes to mind, running in place in midair, then hunching his shoulders to his ears before plummeting to the canyon.

In slow motion, the nose of the plane drops. For a second, it's level. Then it points, then it points down into the clouds and the shifting green mass barely discernible way below. Tina locks her knees together, as if she might squeeze gravity between them. The plane is angled toward the ground. It's going down.

Unbelievably, Marv pushes the stick forward, giving the engine gas. This is his revenge on her mercenary mother, this suicide with daughter in tow. How odd it will be, she thinks irrelevantly, for people to find the jumble of caplets, the neatly measured Baggies in her suitcase, after the crash and the funeral. The engine roars to life. Screams rise in Tina's throat.

They rush through the gray clouds, blinded. Then Tina sees

the trees below, the hills. Then the nose lifts, the wings straighten. They are flying. Her knees unlock. Marv throttles down.

"It's okay," he says to Tina as she starts to weep. "We're fine, now. Just a regular stall. Fine, fine."

But she can't stop it, the weeping. All the way through the easy landing, the taxi to the hangar outside Little Rock, the drive home in Marvin's quiet Lincoln, the tears pour from Tina's eyes.

"Just nerves," Marvin says to her, and she repeats it, "Just nerves," but still she can't stop. Me and the baby too, she wants to tell him, it was both of us falling.

"Had to accelerate," Marvin explains to Elaine while Tina descends to mix her brew downstairs.

Squatting between the twin beds of the guest room on the lower floor, Tina immerses the coil. She looks out the window while she waits. This is not the house she grew up in. It's set on a rise by an artificial lake populated by wild geese. For exercise and escape, Tina often walks the perimeter of the lake, though the thick scattering of goose droppings gives the landscape a crusted, infertile look.

Through the thin ceiling come voices and the heavy *kerlug, kerlug* of Marvin's tread as he heads over to the bar in the den. "It was nothing to worry over!" he says.

"You practically killed her!" Her mother's voice trembles, deep with smoke.

"Just a stall. You have to do maybe three dozen of them to get out of flight school. You should see the ones over the tail." *Kerlug, kerlug.* Marvin has bad knees.

"You did this to get at me."

"Don't be insane."

Their voices rasp on. They make Tina tired, right through to her fingers and toes. Slowly, when she's swallowed the brew, she pulls off her socks and dusty shoes, and stretches out on the bed. She doesn't blame Marv for the stall, the terror. She blames no one for anything. Before she shuts her eyes, she glances at the clock. An hour at least before dinner, before they come snooping after her.

Asleep, Tina dreams of stalking a stranger through an abandoned warehouse, finally killing it, with lots of blood. She wakes knowing someone else is in the room. She opens her eyes to Elaine sitting cross-legged on the matching twin bed, smoking a cigarette. "Supper?" Tina says. She lifts her head, then lets it sink back onto the pillow.

"It's keeping warm," says Elaine. "I had to get away from him." She gives a little shiver, then leans over her knees. "I'm hiding," she says.

"You guys are fighting a lot," says Tina. She shuts her eyes: the warehouse, the blood. Whom has she killed?

"Marvin is an alcoholic," says her mother.

"I thought he was supposed to be funny."

Elaine drags on her cigarette, the tip glowing in the dark. "You know what I would like to do?" she asks.

"No," says Tina. She lies like a prone statue, the way she always used to when her mother came into her room late at night. If you lie still long enough, she used to tell herself, you can pretend it's all a dream, the kind that rolls by like a movie.

"I would like," Elaine says, stabbing the cigarette into the ashtray on the bedside table, "to cut off his balls."

"God," Tina says. She shuts her eyes. The bed is a ship, absolutely stable, even on the high seas.

"I would like to cut them off, cook them, and eat them."

Tina opens her eyes. Carefully, horribly, her mother is working her jaw. Tina shuts her eyes again. "Pizzazz," people always say of her mother. "That girl's got pizzazz." She pictures Elaine cooking fat Marvin's tender balls, serving them up on a platter, good husband material sprinkled with pizzazz.

"I've got to take a shower," she says.

Leaving Elaine on the spare bed, Tina steps across the narrow hall into the bathroom. She does need a shower. She's been taking two a day. Always she feels the need to rinse off. Maybe it's the herbs. Afterwards she's been drying in front of the electric heater, her hair wrapped in a thick towel while she brushes her teeth over the shell-shaped washbasin, to get the taste of the poison out. She shuts and locks the door. This bathroom has full-length mirrors on both walls. Standing in between, she runs her hands over her breasts and belly. There's hardly any change. If she hadn't had the test to confirm it, she might have fooled herself for another couple of weeks. The clinician was efficient and kind, a West Indian nurse who took Tina's thirty-five dollars and then washed her hands. She told Tina to call that day between five-thirty and six.

Tina sinks down on the pink oval bathroom rug, leans back against the mirror, shuts her eyes. It's a big, rich house, this house. The geese outside honk at dawn; light ricochets off the lake. She'll miss coming here. Her mother will leave it, when she leaves Marvin. Tina remembers the first man her mother dated after the divorce. He wasn't rich, like Marvin, but he was running for mayor. That was the year Little Rock had the highest incidence of reported rape cases in the nation, and her mother's boyfriend had gleefully explained it to the press. "Why?" he asked, rhetorically. "'Cause we got the prettiest girls here, that's why."

Knock on the bathroom door: Elaine. "Don't dawdle, dearie," she says. "Theater."

"Just a quick shower, Mom."

"I didn't mean that," Elaine says through the door.

"I know you didn't," says Tina.

She runs the water hot, then steps in. It's almost six, just about the hour she made the call, from the subway platform at Eighty-Sixth Street, down to the clinic. "Positive!" the clinician had reported, shouting at her, as a train roared into the station. "D'you want an appointment?"

"For what?" Tina had yelled back.

"To decide!"

"No!" Tina shouted just as the train stood still. Her voice echoed in the cold station.

"Beg pardon, Miss!"

Tina had hung up, dizzy, and leaned against the pay phone. For a moment, she shut her eyes and drew in the stench of urine, the hot rubber of the subway cars. When she opened her eyes, it had been something like the way it was this afternoon, in the plane—everything tilted the wrong way, a sudden silence where there should have been noise. Then there was a man shouting at her that other people had to use the phone.

Ashley would say, if Tina asked her, that Tina had just been a little careless. Carefree, they used to call it. In the Sixties, before Tina was even born. Oh, to be careful, like her mother— upstairs, now, victorious in the harsh tinkle of her laughter. To shop for husband material. To partner yourself to men who say those things—the prettiest girls, mighty cold cunt—and it has nothing to do with you. Was that what the Sixties had killed? All the good husband material?

She flicks the faucets off. The bathroom's steamy, and she doesn't want to run the fan. Her legs feel like rubber, her belly like a water balloon. The preparation's settling on her empty stomach, the rich herbs and finely ground roots. "Does it happen all at once," Tina had asked Ashley when she got the recipe from her, "or like a period, gradual at first?"

"Depends, I guess." Ashley had written the recipe out in her neat cursive on hay-colored handmade paper and taped a tiny square of dark chocolate to the bottom, to make Tina feel better. "I use it so much, I'm not sure which is a period and which an abortion, to tell the truth."

Ashley helped out the first time Tina proved herself careless, a year ago. She was there to run the gauntlet with Tina between the outstretched hands and pamphlets. Afterwards she supplied Tina with blackberry brandy and brought her a tape of Portuguese music, guitar chords to ease her pain. Tina didn't want, then, to try Ashley's poison. This time, she can't bear the alternative: the photos of dead babies thrust at her, their weak limbs and astonishing heads, the smock and the little room, the suction.

"Tina!" her mother is calling from upstairs. "Dinner!"

"On my way!" says Tina. She dries and dresses, a soft beige sweater and green skirt, around her neck a silver amulet she bought at Warlock Wisdom. Crouching to her suitcase, she puts away the immerser and the cracked mug. Lennon gazes dolefully at her. The herbs are secure in the zippered pocket. As she straightens up, Tina's hips twinge. "Oh," she says aloud. Like a snake, the pain darts to the front of her abdomen and punches her. "Oh!" Before she can take a step, sure enough, the sensation of dampness in her panties.

She hobbles to the bathroom. She hadn't thought of pads. Ah, the hospitable Elaine: a stack of pink Kotex in the second drawer. A swipe at the thighs and protection in place.

But it isn't enough. She's barely lain down on the bed before she needs another.

"Tina!" Elaine's voice is more shrill now. Elaine cannot bear tardiness. She loves the theater.

Tina pushes herself off the bed. "Sorry, Mom! Sec!"

Another stop at the bathroom. Double pad, this time. She'll never make the theater. She'll have to claim a headache, a delayed reaction to the flying fiasco. The little wastebasket in the bathroom looks to be filling with dead animals. She starts up the stairs.

"Hey, girlie," says Marvin from the top step. Tina looks up. How sweet and sad he looks, this husband material, and how far away. His lips move, saying something more, but she can't quite hear it. She clutches her amulet, lifts her foot to the next step.

Inside her a voice is roaring, like the radio on Marv's plane, unintelligible. As she listens, Tina can feel the poison taking effect. It will do it—will tear up her womb. She can almost mark its measure, the way she marked the pull of gravity on the nose of Marvin's plane. Pushing the throttle against sense, she lifts her other foot.

"Elaine!" Marv's voice punctuates the clouds. As Tina plummets, he stumbles with his bad knees down the stairs and catches her. And then there is Elaine, and by the two of them Tina is borne up, torn and bleeding, into their healing arms.

Safe-T-Man

For D.F.B.

Safe-T-Man is six feet tall and has ethnically ambiguous skin and features. He can stand all night in the doorway, or you can bend his hips and knees to make him sit in an armchair or at the kitchen table, where he is now. Lucille left him disassembled in his box until one afternoon, a week after Carol moved onto the campus, when the two of them finished a bottle of Ouzo and put him together. Although the cover of the box had shown him in a beige cap and black sunglasses, he arrived with no clothes and expressionless eyes, a staring brown.

Today Lucille and Carol have dressed him as Bogart, fedora and raincoat, underneath which they've mischievously strapped a red bra and garter belt, trimmed in black lace. Safe-T-Man, as Lucille and Carol both noticed the moment they unwrapped his separate parts, is anatomically incomplete.

Carol and Lucille both live on Professors' Row, a countrified lane above the main quad of the Lutheran women's college where they work. Lucille—Lucy Lee, to the local Southerners— teaches modern dance, which the girls take because they think it's easier than ballet. "I think Roy and I'll get divorced, this year," was what she told Carol in her jazzed-up drawl, the week Carol moved in; but it's been over a year, now, and Roy keeps coming up on weekends, so it isn't looking like divorce to Carol. Roy's a woodworker who caretakes a farm; Carol's husband, Gerald, was a stock analyst, before things came apart.

It's late in the afternoon, and Carol's pouring herself a glass of wine in the hope of being able to sleep, later. Her six-year-old, Chris, is playing Nintendo in the living room with Lucille's son Alex; the littler ones are down for a nap on Lucille's bed. "I used to have fantasies that Roy had up and died," Lucille is saying. "In his sleep or something, a heart condition we never knew about, painless and he's gone. Then I wouldn't have to feel guilty about anything."

"They say," says Carol, "that the death of a parent is a lot less traumatic than divorce." She takes a drag on Lucille's cigarette. Lucille's been getting bouts of diarrhea, and claims that smoking helps stop it. "They say it's not the parent's absence but all the tension that screws kids up. Statistically."

"Well, Roy's absence might screw Alex up, a little. But he'd straighten out in a week or so."

"Do you have a life insurance policy?"

"No."

"We do," says Carol. "Three hundred thousand dollars. When things were really bad, back in Boston, I thought maybe I'd torture Gerald so much, that with his depression and all he'd go off and commit suicide. Only he'd do it in a way where we'd still get the three hundred thousand. You know, like a car accident. I used to think what a sweet thing that would be for him to do."

"Alex!" Lucille calls out. There's a skirmish going on over Mario Brothers. "You share, now!"

"It's Chris's fault," says Carol, moving to the kitchen door. "He just plays with Alex because Alex has Super Nintendo."

"Oh, I don't care. You know I don't care."

Chris has yanked the controller away and is holding it high over his head, with Alex clawing at his arm. "I'm counting to three," says Carol. At two her son hands the gadget over, shooting her the same look she gets from her husband when she restacks the dishwasher.

"When Gerald had a job and traveled to Connecticut," Carol says, coming back to the kitchen table, "I used to think what if he had an affair."

"Oh, adultery, I'm into that big time," says Lucille. "Catch him at it. Then no matter what I did, I'd be justified. But Roy never would."

"No," sighs Carol. "Gerald neither. I wonder," she adds, sipping her wine, "if it would be easier or harder, really, without them. On the practical level, I mean."

"Look, even though these kids are going to drive me cuckoo by tonight," says Lucille, "you couldn't get me to live with that man full-time."

"Well, what's the point then? Of all the traipsing back and forth, keeping two houses?"

"I don't know," says Lucille. She gets up to check on both their babies. "For the love of God, I don't know."

But Carol, dragging her kids home later that afternoon, knows. Lucille really loves her husband, in a begrudging way. Why shouldn't she? Just two weeks ago he came roaring in at seven in the morning with a truckload of oak pieces, and through the day he assembled a new bed for Lucille to sleep in these nights while she's away from him, earning money teaching Lutheran girls to plié. Carol finds the bed in bad taste—the oak's too thick, too polished, and above the headboard there's a grotesque branch arching out, with gigantic wooden daisies stemming from it. But Lucille's delighted, calls it her "bower." At least it shows some devotion, is what Carol concedes. The man is a woodworker; he has a calling. Whereas Gerald, since the firing—well, most of the time Carol has herself convinced she's just waiting for the right opportunity.

Across the road, Gerald is pulling game hens out of the oven. "So much meat," Carol says.

"It's something I know how to cook." Carefully Gerald

bastes the birds, tucks them back in, and checks on a pot of boiling water.

"Noodles?" Carol asks.

"Angel hair."

"Well, Chris'll eat that, at least. He doesn't *like* meat," she reminds Gerald when he looks quizzical. "*None* of us like meat," she adds.

"Your loss," he says coolly. "Lissa napped?"

"Yeah, darn it," says Carol. "She'll be up till ten. Did you get Pull-Ups?" she asks, knowing he hasn't. Gerald doesn't want to admit that Lissa still wets her bed.

"Forgot," he says.

"I don't need Pull-Ups!" calls Lissa from the living room, where she's spilled a puzzle onto the floor. "I'm big girl!"

"You're a big girl who has accidents sometimes," says Carol. "Want me to help you with that?"

"No. You *watch.*"

"Dinner in five minutes," says Gerald from the kitchen. "The children should be setting the table."

"Oh, Christ." Carol rolls her eyes at her daughter, who giggles. "She's just started the puzzle, honey," she says. "You know how she gets if she can't finish."

"Five minutes," says Gerald.

"God in heaven. Chris!" Carol calls, knowing she won't get an answer. Whenever they come home, Chris goes straight to his room and shuts the door, and launches into imaginary combat. *Take that, Green Ranger! Zzvvaap! Pschow! Come in Zordon!*

Pushing open the door, Carol finds her son leaping from his bed to Lissa's, thrusting his arms out in front of him like switchblades flashing. She stands there for twenty seconds, wishing life were very, very different. During a moment of silence she steps into the room. "Pause, Chris," she says. "Put the game on pause and help me out here."

His brown hair disheveled, her handsome son looks at her

as if through the pinhole of a kaleidoscope. "I can't pause," he says. "I'm at the fourth level."

Carol considers reminding Chris that he is not inside a TV set, but discards the idea. "Then you've got two bosses still to beat anyway," she says instead. "Better to save your strength. You'll get a half-hour of pretend after supper."

"I want to play with Alex then!"

"We'll talk about it. But only if you help me. If you do not help me," she adds in a lower voice, leaning into the room, "your father will throw a fit. *Capische?*"

It's not fair, she knows, but that threat always gets his cooperation.

"Okay, Mom," says Chris, shrugging and jumping down from the bed.

Family dinner is one thing Gerald insists on, now that he's in charge. Back in Boston, when he worked late evenings, Carol would feed the kids Ninja Turtle Pasta and carrot strips; she'd eat leftover Chinese after they went down. So much calmer, she thinks as she wrestles Chris and Lissa toward the dining room. But somehow they manage the evening. Nobody mentions TV or Alex, and bathtime rolls around without complaint.

Granted, Carol hasn't managed to take the pressure off her husband. Days like this, when she's spent time with Lucille, she tends to be crueler. She can't stand how contented Gerald seems, living at this little college, playing with Chris and baby Lissa, cooking his favorite dish for supper, reading the New York *Times* that Carol's picked up at the college bookstore and never got to herself. Carol is a journalist; she can't get herself to say "professor of journalism," yet. Back in Boston, she had a regular column on the *Phoenix* and did lengthy, investigative articles.

"So," she says to Gerald over the game hens, "I figure you read the paper top to bottom today. Fill me in on the primaries. Unless you happen to have spent time with the employment section."

And later, when she can't find toilet paper, "I wish you'd check before you go to the market. Every month we run out."

"Thought I'd bought a lifetime supply!" he calls from the bedroom where he's puttering.

"With you *home* all the time it goes fast."

And finally, as if enough weren't enough, she noisily puts away all the junk that's been left strewn around the front hall while Gerald reads a story to the kids.

"Your turn," he calls.

"All right," she says. Taking a last look at the front hall she adds, in an audible undertone, "Pigsty."

When she reaches the kids' bedroom door, she knows from his face that the whisper's done it, the last straw, and she has the familiar, momentary impulse to take back every bitchy remark. She would say, if she let herself: "I know you try, and you stay cheerful, and you took my bike in to be fixed today and you remembered to pick up conditioner and tampons for me at the store and you haven't got friends to talk to." But he'll use it, she knows, and so she pinches her lips together, trapping her conciliatory words. "If you're not going to wear a Pull-Up, Lissa," she says instead, turning her attention to the bedroom, "you need an extra pee before night night."

"I'm going out," says Gerald, behind her.

"Really?"

"Yeah. Down to the Rat, I think."

The Rat, Rathaus, is where the students gather. There's live music, sometimes. The students bring their Lutheran boyfriends from the college ten miles away and sit there drinking Snapple and tapping their feet. Faculty don't go there. This is Gerald's third time.

"Well," says Carol, "have fun."

After she has tucked the kids in and graded papers and read the scattered *Times* and even sifted through her files for an article she keeps meaning to write about female militia members, Carol gets antsy. She drinks a glass of wine. She even flicks on HBO, which is showing *The Silence of the Lambs*. At eleven she calls Lucille. "Can I borrow Safe-T-Man?" she asks.

"What, you proving something to Gerald?"

"Gerald's gone out."

"Where?"

"Dunno."

"*Ohhh.* Well sure, darling. Whatever makes you cozy. Come get him, though, I'm standing here dripping."

"Sorry."

"You know I don't care."

Carol quickly checks the kids, then races out the door, across the road, and into Lucille's kitchen, where she grabs Safe-T-Man around the chest and under one arm and hauls him, still in a seated posture, out the door. "Thanks!" she calls over her shoulder as she sets him down on the walk to shut the door behind her. Then she carries him, football-style, across the road. He is surprisingly light.

Back at her house, Chris and Lissa haven't stirred. Carol carts Safe-T-Man to the living room, sets him on the futon, removes the fedora, and gives him yesterday's newspaper to read. There you sit, she thinks, my husband. But you don't have to dress that way, you know. We could change you. Put you in overalls and hand you a lunch pail, you're off to your shift. Put you in corduroys and turtleneck, you're out helping the homeless for ten grand a year.

Something will come up, he says.

No, it won't! Things don't come up in life anymore, Gerald. That's your view.

My view, nothing. You're vanishing before my eyes. You're just a shirt and pants, and nothing on the inside.

"Who you talking to, Mom?" comes Chris's light voice.

Good God, she's been talking aloud. After a little jump of

surprise Carol gets up and puts her arm around him, standing in the hallway rubbing his eyes.

"Just practicing something, honey," she says. "You need a drink of water?"

He looks at Safe-T-Man as she leads him back to his room, but he doesn't ask about it. He knows his mom and Lucille share things. He knows this is just a big doll.

When Chris is down, Carol puts away her wine glass. Before she flicks off the living room light, she moves Safe-T-Man closer to the window. From a distance, he's supposed to look formidable, like a militia man; that's why Lucille's mother sent him. But up close, she wonders what cat burglar or rapist would be scared. There is something ambiguous about the tuck of his chin, or maybe it's the delicate fingers on his fawn-colored hands. He'll protect her, the children, but he's more vulnerable than people think.

Running a bath as hot as she can, she sprinkles lavender salts, then steps gingerly into it, and finally slides down to where her hair floats around her face and only her head is out of the water. For ten minutes she thinks kind, gentle thoughts. She's pulling herself out of the tub when she hears steps in the hallway and knows that Gerald is home.

"Hey," she says as he opens the bathroom door. Towels wrap her torso and head. "You were out late." Her voice comes out almost sultry. The bath has relaxed her, made her feel watched over.

"Sorry."

His face looks off-kilter; she smells beer. She wonders if he saw Safe-T-Man from outside, if he had a momentary shock. "No, no," she says. "Did you have fun?"

In his shoes, his hair unkempt, he looks down at her strangely, as if she's just started talking in a foreign tongue. "I didn't go to the Rat."

"Where, then?"

"I spent time," he says slowly, eyes unflinching, "with Jenny."

"Jenny?"

"You heard me. A student. Three weeks, now, I've been seeing her. And I need a shower." He starts to push past her, rudely, but she puts her hand on his arm. It's his arm, still, same shape and musculature.

"Wait," she says. Holding the towel across her breasts so it doesn't fall off, she leans down toward his groin. She sniffs. "Jesus," she says, straightening up. "You have. You do."

She's supposed to be angry. But this is Gerald, standing so close to her—his Roman nose with the slight kink in it from an old break, the mole on his neck, the loose set of his hips. She can't go from *Gerald* to *unfaithful husband* quick enough to spark anger. In fact, the weird thing is that he looks beat and she has the impulse to put her arms around him, as if she were old and wise and he were her grown son. So that's what she does.

"Don't," he says, shaking her off. The towel falls. He turns, flicks the shower on, peels off his shirt. Underneath, the same chest, a few gray hairs among the black. He glares at her. "Divorce me if you want," he says, "but leave me my privacy here, please."

"What?"

"I want you to get out of the bathroom, Carol."

She shrugs. "Okey-doke." Outside, the hallway is unexpectedly cool. She thinks about kicking the bathroom door—her bathrobe's in there—but doesn't. Quickly, in the dark bedroom, she pulls on nightgown and slippers. She combs out her hair. Then she pours herself a glass of brandy in the kitchen and goes to sit with Safe-T.

He's done it, she tells him.

And he answers, not looking up, What did you expect?

Minutes tick by on the mantel clock. From the bathroom comes the distant waterfall of Gerald's shower. Carol can't read or look at the militia file anymore; her hands are too shaky. Then, slowly, she lets herself be hypnotized: by the clock's motion, by the rough sounds of six-year-old Chris sleeping in the next room. She's remembering the one guy who's made a bona fide pass at her since she's been married: the former op-ed editor at the city paper, one of those gray eminences who try to make you think you're the only one they've ever hit on like this. It was after a reception for a bunch of foreign journalists. He followed her when she went to fetch a tray of vegetables from the little kitchen at the press club, and there he half-led, half-pushed her into the pantry. With her back to the refrigerator where they kept the beer, he pressed his whole length up against her.

The mantel clock gives that extra tick which means the hour hand has moved. One o'clock. Snapping out of it, Carol goes to find her husband asleep in bed, his hair still wet, his mouth making much the same gruffling sound as his son's only more spasmodic. She takes a blanket back to the living room and puts her head on Safe-T's lap, to weep. But she knows Safe-T is wide awake, always awake, and that makes her nervous. Finally she stumbles down the hall to her room and her accustomed place, and after a couple of hours she takes a pill and drifts off.

"How was our boy?" Lucille asks the next day.

"Which one?"

"Safe-T, of course. I saw your husband weave up the road, I *know* how he is."

For a second Carol's confused, then she realizes Lucille just means drunk, she noticed Gerald was drunk. "Safe-T was great," she says. "We discussed media bashing and Rupert Murdoch. He's really very informed for someone in his profession."

"Yeah, well you can keep him for the weekend. Roy's coming up."

"That's great."

"Yeah, maybe he'll have a car wreck on the way."

Carol doesn't tell her about Gerald sleeping with the student. Later, taking Lissa to preschool, she can't figure why she didn't. She's not ashamed—it's what she and Lucille have been fantasizing about—and she doesn't think Lucille will broadcast the news. But she'll want to know how Carol feels about it, and Carol can't say yet. She's not upset any more, but not thrilled either. She's curious. She realizes with a little start, backing her car out of the Montessori parking lot, that what she wants more than anything is to see Gerald with this Jenny person. She doesn't *see* him, when he's making love to her. He's a blur of face and chest, flesh and hair, and a sensation inside of her. She wants to know how he acts, as a lover apart from her. It's the only identity he's acquired since he lost his job and they moved.

She's got just one class that morning—Cultural Reportage—and she knows Gerald's routine by now. At noon she heads up the hill on the back path, so she arrives at her house by way of the woods. Crouched between a rhododendron and a white dogwood, she waits. Sure enough, too good to be real, Gerald emerges through the kitchen door. He drops a bag of trash in the bin then starts off for his daily walk. He's wearing an old polo shirt and dark shorts, and Carol thinks what good shape he's in. Careful to make it look accidental if she's caught, she follows him at a distance.

He goes the way he always goes—by the old barn, down around the gym complex, out over the stretch that runs across the creek and then alongside it as far as the college gates. Then he turns toward the Creek Houses, odd-looking redwood "modules" up on stilts, set into the hill. They're where the seniors live, eight or ten in a module, as close as the college has come to experimental living. Carol holds her breath by the bridge as her husband strides around the first Creek House and then disappears inside.

For a few minutes, Carol is a statue: Safe-T-Woman. What's left to discover? Then she's crouched, crabwalking. Let no students approach.

A flat rock juts alongside the Creek House. Above it, at eye level, two tall narrow windows. A woman's shape has just traversed one, on her way to answer a knock. Carol can make out her high breasts, the sweep of her brown hair. She doesn't know this Jenny. Must not take any journalism. Art major, maybe; those were always the ones.

She shuffles out onto the rock. The windowsill is at her nose, but if she steps back she'll fall into the water. The Creek House is so shoddily constructed, she can feel Gerald's footsteps through the outer wall. But the best she can do, for peeping, is to tip her head back and catch a glimpse of a dresser mirror on Jenny's wall. She feels like a rock climber, ready to hammer a piton. The mirror reflects the ceiling light and the top of a head, Gerald's head.

They are talking. She feels more than hears the voices. Pitch and fall, pitch and fall. Gerald is apologizing—for being late, for being rough last night, for being whatever and whoever he is. The girl's voice sounds surprised. Of course: This would not be a planned meeting. It's too soon. They hooked up last night. *Hooked up*, Carol likes that expression. The students use it, as if sex were no more than crooking pinkie fingers with one another. So will they hook up again, now?

She presses her ear to the wall. Can make out no words. Only the high lilt of the girl's voice, like chatter on a radio, and then the thumps of Gerald's words and shoes, at the same time. Well, what if Carol could distinguish words? She's got no notepad, no tape recorder. Some investigative journalist she is. Shutting her eyes, she leans against the rough siding of the Creek House.

Funny—from the simple punctuation of Gerald's voice, she can picture the expression on his face. A deep, sad wrinkle cuts

between his eyebrows, more to the left than the right—the way
he looked when they had to put the dog down, just after Chris
was born. He took it hard, losing that dog. She feels a rush of
love for him.

Now it's the girl's voice—throatier—and the girl's footsteps.
They are definitely not making love. Not that Gerald would be
silent. The first time he made love to Carol, he spun skeins of
words around her; the next morning her throat was raw, from
kissing sucking talking talking. But the muffled, unintelligible
human sounds that Carol is picking up are still flying across the
air of the room. Gerald's footsteps reverberate again, heading
toward the door.

Carol's eyes fly open. She looks across the creek. At a distance, perhaps two hundred paces away, a trio of girls is fast-
walking the campus circuit, their long hair tied back in high
ponytails, their pale thighs girdled in neon Lycra. They'll see her.
No, they *have* seen her, the journalism prof, the one who assigns
papers on lesbian politics, snooping around student housing. No.
They haven't even glanced over. She ducks, she leaps. Off the
flat rock onto the ragged ground. If she heads around the front
of the Creek House, they'll never see her. But Gerald. Earnestly,
she jogs the other way, not over but past the bridge and into the
scant woods. The students power-walk on by.

Then Gerald emerges, brushes back his hair, a man who's
slipped the noose. Crouched in the woods, Carol imagines full-
breasted Jenny, alone, slamming the flat of her hand against the
wall of her ill-constructed dorm room. Gerald shoves his hands
into his pockets, strolls the bridge. He hasn't seen Carol. Or else
he has—they all have—and they're just playing along, the way
she does when Lissa hides behind the curtains with her feet
sticking out.

As soon as Gerald has rounded the bend, Carol short-cuts
home through the campus. Let Jenny be watching her too,
through the obelisk of her window, she doesn't care. Once she's

past the first academic building, she jogs the rest of the way. There, in the living room, she paces, awaiting her husband. Safe-T-Man hasn't moved from behind his newspaper, but she addresses him anyway.

"That's Gerald's strength, you know," she says aloud. "How he manages to slide in and then out of a situation. He could do that with investments. He'd been doing it for ages with women before he met me. You're not *listening,*" she says, stepping over to him. She pulls the newspaper out of his molded hands. Then she picks him up and carries him to the bedroom. "You need a change," she tells him. Peeling off the clothes from Lucille, she dresses him in one of Gerald's old suits—summer weight, a light grey, with a geometric tie in shades of rose. No women's clothing. "Sit here," she says, plunking him in the armchair in the corner of the room. "Record the proceedings."

Late that night, after Lucille calls, Carol brings Safe-T-Man back. "I'm just kinda nervous," Lucille said on the phone. "Roy said he was leaving at two, it only takes three hours. Am I being stupid?"

"'Course not," Carol said.

She's left Gerald snoring. Wrapped in a robe, Safe-T under her arm, she finds Lucille chain-smoking, her baby Benjamin asleep in her lap.

"He was colicky from seven on," Lucille says. "If I put him down he'll just start up again."

"You don't look so great yourself." Carol lights a cigarette and pours herself warm white wine.

"Well, it was bad, it was bad this morning. I was driving this one to his babysitter's—you'll love this, Carol—and I got this stab of diarrhea pain. Like a dagger, I thought I was going to throw up. Throw up or shit in the car, I didn't know which, and I've got to drop him and get to class, and so I stop in the Texaco station and I keep him strapped in his seat while I run into the restroom and I have these major runs."

"Nerves."

"Plus it's my period."

"Oh, shit. So to speak."

"So I finish unloading all this into the toilet and then I look up and of course they have no fucking toilet paper! Nothing at all."

"And you have nothing."

"I've locked my fucking purse in the car with Benjamin. So then you know what I do. I take off my fucking underwear."

"And you roll it up after, right?"

"No. After I use it I flush it down the toilet."

"What about your period?"

"I've got a used Kleenex in the car. Right there in the driver's seat I wad it up and shove it in under my skirt. Then I take Benjy to the sitter and go teach dance. That's how bad it is."

"Well, practical, really."

"It is going to kill me, the way we live."

"Of course it is," says Carol. She gets up and strokes baby Benjamin's fine web of hair, then goes to the window. In the reflecting glass she can see the happy family: Safe-T-Man in his business suit, Lucille exhausted, sleeping babe. "Do you think he's okay?" she asks.

"Who, Roy? I hope he drove the truck into the Sewanee River."

"No, you don't."

"All right, I fucking don't, but he can't pull this shit on me. Pass me my cigarettes."

"You know what I did this afternoon?" Carol says, lighting Lucille's cigarette from her own and then blowing the smoke against the window.

"Broke the Nintendo? Threw out Lissa's diapers?"

"No. I was late picking Chris up because I was screwing my husband."

"Hey, what'd he do, get a job?"

"No. He's as empty as ever." Carol presses her face against the window. Down the hill, she can make out the symmetrical lights of the dorm rooms, where the Lutheran girls sprawl on their bunk beds and gossip into the wee hours. "I pretended Gerald was the drug fiend I'd taken as a lover," she says to Lucille. "And my husband here"—she nods toward Safe-T-Man—"had to watch it all."

"That's an interesting concept. God, I have the shits again. Here, hold Benjamin." Lucille hands the baby over and struggles up from the rocking chair where she's been sitting. Carol cradles him, heavy and warm. At first, while Lucille's in the bathroom, she just walks him around the living room, humming. Then she steps to the back door.

"Now, don't you let anything happen," she says to Safe-T, who's sitting smug and eunuch-like at the table.

He nods, and she takes Benjamin outside, where there's a warm breeze blowing, freshening the air. That afternoon, when Gerald came, he cried "Baby sweet!" which isn't anything he's ever called Carol, was meant indeed for the ghost of Jenny. Chris, when he got over being picked up late, exacted an extra round of MegaMan Plus, and spent the early evening practicing karate leaps from the cherry tree. Lissa is right now in bed without a Pull-Up. They all imagine themselves more capable than they are. She, Carol, has a right to imagine herself in love with her husband. It's only fair.

"Where are you?" she hears Lucille's voice calling from inside. As Carol turns to bring Benjamin back in, she sees truck lights, rounding the bend at the bottom of the hill.

Could be Roy, she'll tell Lucille.

Time-Share

For V.B.

Tony Romeo had been a third baseman, and not a bad one. Ben whispered that he'd seen him in the headlines, ten years back, for the double play that turned the World Series over to the Padres. He walked with a ball player's swagger, as if he still had his cup on. His shoulders pulled at the seams of his Barney's jacket. Jill spent no small amount of time studying his exceptionally large, plump earlobes, the right with a distinct dimple toward the center that moved as Tony talked.

Right now, he was talking about Hawaii. "This place on Oahu," he said, "is truly spectacular. Look at the map here. Steps to the golf course. You golf?"

"I've golfed on Oahu," said Ben. "There's one fabulous place, on the other end of the island, with a par of ninety-seven and a volcano behind the ninth hole."

"Yeah, yeah. I *know* that course."

"Do you?"

"This one's better, though. I had a share in this building, see, for five years. Phenomenal place."

They both looked at Jill. It was her turn. "I bet," she said.

Ben did golf, though of course she'd never seen him at it. It irritated her that he should play this game so well, encouraging the small, dim light far back in Romeo's brain that he might for once, just this once, land a sale. They were sitting in a peach-colored cubicle somewhere on the fourteenth floor, in an annex of the hotel reserved for these shenanigans. In front of Tony lay a group of glossy brochures filled with tiny pictures of high-rise buildings backed by blue skies and rated according to their swimming pools and exchangeability. In front of Ben and Jill sat small notepads on which they resolutely did not doodle, and twin glasses filled with Perrier.

"And you can stay here," Tony pressed on, "any time you like. There's a waiting list of five years for this particular location, but with your points, you can stay here given, say, two weeks' notice. It's phenomenal."

"Fabulous," said Ben. His hand found Jill's thigh.

"Do you mean to tell me," Jill said, pulling the brochure slightly closer, "that there are units in this place just lying empty, waiting for a phone call from New York?"

"That's not exactly how it works," said Tony patiently.

"Well, I don't see how else it can work. If we're going to call up and say, 'Give us an apartment for a week,' there has to be something available."

"There are things available. Which is not to say they are empty when you call," said Tony. "It's a complicated system."

"I'll explain it to you later, honey," said Ben, and his hand gave a small squeeze. She stroked the back of it, the few wiry hairs that trickled down from his wrist.

"Dare you," she said. They looked at each other, then turned back to Romeo, who was refusing to appear disconcerted—even though wet patches had blossomed under his arms, where the jacket hung open.

"Where else do you folks like to vacation?" he tried. "Europe? The Riviera? You strike me as a Europe-type woman," he said to Jill.

"Europe, sure," she said. She ran her fingers through her just-cut hair, an inch all around and moussed with something that smelled like blackberries. "We've never been to Europe together."

"Look what we got here. Coast of Spain. This is a five-star place, just like Manhattan Mews. So you got an even swap here. We're talking two swimming pools, in-house masseur, 24-hour wet bar. You don't like Spain? Here we've got Brittany. Very Old World. Look how charming this courtyard is. Private courtyard. Fifteen stories."

Jill was beginning to feel sick. Tony Romeo was showing them abominations, and they were acting interested. All for a dirt-cheap honeymoon suite in midtown Manhattan, all because he had them by the balls.

Tony Romeo was not stupid. Forty-five minutes ago he'd swaggered into the Manhattan Mews reception area, where Jill and Ben were waiting along with the other opportunistic week-enders. After shaking hands—Tony's was large, of course, and unnecessarily creamy—Jill had mentioned that Tony was a half-hour late and she had an appointment downtown at three. They would have to cut the time-share presentation short, she'd said. In that case, Tony said kindly, he would refuse to do it. And yes, then Jill and Ben would owe the retail price of their two nights' stay, which was five hundred dollars. Crocodile-like, he had smiled. Jill had said, Well, on consideration she could change her appointment. Tony had said the attitude wasn't good, he wasn't sure he could do the presentation at all. Nonsense, Ben had said, adding his own oily grin to the equation, we're extremely keen on the whole time-share option. Just got off on a wrong foot, is all.

But they were on notice.

"So," said Tony now, shifting his substantial weight in the padded chair and drawing forth the form the computer had spat out, "You two are—?"

"Are what?" said Ben, blinking. He had a way of blinking rapidly when he wasn't quite in control of a conversation, a habit that used to bother Jill.

"You are married, or living together, or—"

"Just partners," Jill said quickly.

"Hm. How long you been together?"

"How long's it been, honey?" Jill asked.

"I dunno. Year and a half?" said Ben, turning toward her. His hand came off her knee. "Two years?"

"Almost two years, I think." David had turned three, Karen was cutting baby teeth. Two years ago Jill's husband, Roger, was just starting to renovate their house outside Syracuse, and Jill had never heard Ben's name.

"And which one's the installation artist?" said Tony.

"I am," Jill said. She slipped her left foot out of her black pump and placed it on Ben's instep.

"What line of work is that?"

"You build big pieces," Jill said, "and install them in a specific place."

"Kinda like a—a contractor."

"Kind of." She felt Ben's foot pushing against hers.

"The things women can do these days." Tony wagged his head toward Ben, who turned a palm up. "What about you, Roger?"

"Look on your sheet."

"Financial advisor, it says."

"You got me."

"Great market for it."

"Boom times, yeah."

"So we both," Jill put in, "have flexible schedules."

"Good, good." Tony pulled on one of his outsized earlobes. "That's phenomenal. You'll want to use them, with the shares you can get out of this place. So then. You have a combined income over a hundred thousand."

"What database did you get that from?" Jill said, sitting up a little straighter in her chair.

"It's what they send me from the office. And you've had a time-share before?"

"No!"

Tony looked at her sharply. "It says here that you have. Everyone who got the mailer had."

"Well, not me." She sipped her Perrier, bursting the bubbles with her tongue against the roof of her mouth.

"You've been to a time-share presentation before, then."

"No. Never." Jill swallowed, coloring. As if Tony Romeo knew everything about her. About Ben, known for the afternoon as Roger the financial advisor, sitting next to her.

"I have," said Ben. She rubbed his instep with her bare foot.

"But the flyer didn't come to you," she pointed out.

"Oh, yeah?" big Tony was saying. "Whereabouts?"

"Hawaii. Not your outfit. I can't remember the name of the company."

"You were with him?" Tony said to Jill. His sweat stains were mushrooming.

She shook her head. "Before we knew each other."

"More than two years ago, then."

For a second there was silence, then Ben laughed. "Right, yeah, two years," he said. "You figured that out."

Tony was looking at his hieroglyphic sheet. "But you didn't buy in," he said.

"No."

"Why not?"

"Wasn't the right time. I was thinking of moving, my income was unstable."

"But that's changed now."

"Oh, yeah." Ben wasn't blinking anymore. He was smooth as fudge sauce. "I'm pretty solidly set."

"Looks like," said Tony, with a glance at Jill. He was trying to make up to her.

"It'd be fun," she said, turning to Ben as if she'd been meaning to bring this up, "to take a week in Hawaii together. See your old stomping grounds."

"Make love under the coconut palms," he said.
She fought the color down from her face.
Tony gave a cardboard chuckle. "Just make sure the wind
don't blow a nut down while you're at it," he said. "Ready to see
the real thing?"

He took them up the elevator, around a series of wallpa-
pered corridors, to a one-bedroom furnished apartment with a
chandelier, French doors, reproductions of the French
Impressionists, and a microwave built into the kitchen wall.
There wasn't much to say about the apartment. He showed
them another, Plan B. There wasn't much to say about that one,
either. The choice lay between a large bedroom or a small bedroom plus study; between a bathroom off the bedroom and one
off the dining area. "Real wood," Tony Romeo kept saying. He
offered to show them the meeting rooms.

"I don't think we'd be holding any meetings," said Ben.

He'd laced his fingers with Jill's. Her nerves were quieting.
That morning, before heading out of their hotel room to separate appointments, they had made love twice. Once sleepily, her
mouth furred against his clavicle, her hands cupping his buttocks, his back that much smaller than Roger's so that she could
reach down and across. The second time after finishing flat
champagne, a wordless fucking that had lingered, like a taste in
her mouth, through two meetings with site specialists and lunch
with her agent. This whole scheme—accepting the promotion-
al offer for couples only, substituting Ben for Roger who was
right now, back in Syracuse, picking Karen up at preschool—
had been her brainstorm. She felt the pressure of Ben's fingers,
the strange balance of holding hands with a man almost exactly her height and not quite her weight.

"Take a glance, anyway," said Tony. He looked sorrowful, so
they leaned into a room where blue upholstered conference
chairs tucked into an oval table, not real wood. Tony ticked

"Conference" off on his tour sheet and led them up one more flight, to the lounge.

"You could bring clients here," he said. "More like a private club, really. We stock the *Wall Street Journal*, *Forbes*, you name it."

Jill almost asked what clients Ben might ever have to bring, then remembered. "I already keep a small office in Manhattan," Ben was saying meanwhile. "See most of my New York clients there."

"Oh, yeah? Whereabouts is that?"

"East Thirties. First floor of a renovated brownstone."

"Nice area."

"Fabulous."

Tony cast a quick glance at his printout. Jill pictured the gears grinding. Artist—make that *contractor*—fifty thousand. Total combined income, a hundred ten thousand. Sixty thousand a year and keeping an office in Manhattan, it wouldn't add up. Maybe this Roger, the one Tony was meeting with the Jewish nose and the good pecs, had inheritance money. Kept butch-haired Jill, the big artsy type, as his upstate mistress. When he got the urge to blow some of the inheritance dough in town, he called her and she came in, and they screwed on his great oak desk in the office in the Thirties. Now they would have Manhattan Mews. They would see plays, entertain friends. They would have no children. They would swap for Brittany and stay on the fourteenth floor of the Coast Chateau. They would bring their friends there. Everyone would get a massage. Ben and Jill, the friends would say; Jill and Ben. Thanks for the phenomenal weekend, Bill and Jen.

They were at the lounge. A solitary woman, diminutive, pepper-haired, sat in the middle of the large maroon space sipping Scotch and reading an enormous newspaper.

"Does she own an apartment here?" said Jill.

"Sure, she does. Or she's traded. But like I said," said Tony, "we got ninety-five percent occupancy. Nobody else gets in here."

"She's not a plant, then," said Ben.

"Beg pardon?"

"You didn't hire her, just to sit here reading a newspaper, making us think we might meet someone interesting in the lounge."

Tony looked confused. "No," he said at last. "No, the company wouldn't do that."

"It was a joke," said Ben.

"He's always a tease," said Jill. "Don't mind him."

Roger was a tease. The real Roger, back in Syracuse. Making love, he liked to touch her and then stop, touch and then stop, until she grew exhausted with expectation. She could remember loving Roger, loving the broad set of his shoulders, the gentle way he tended a steak on the grill. The memory of her feelings was sharp and distant at once, like the favorite, half-forgotten smell of a secret closet or Christmas mincemeat. She could not understand that she was betraying him. She tried the words out on herself, but they made no sense either to what she was doing here or to the way she moved about the tall, narrow house in Syracuse, picking up the kids' clothes, watering the many plants.

Ben's situation was simpler. Two years ago, at the High Holy Days, he'd confessed an affair to his wife. Since then they had kept a bitter mistrustful alliance. Ben's wife knew better than to ask where he was staying in New York. The real Roger, on the other hand, called and left messages on the hotel voicemail, Hello, this is the thought police, we're checking on your thoughts of your husband and you are not having enough of them. You have instructions to fantasize.

Jill had never met Ben's children, who were older than hers. She had never tasted his famous Thai cooking. She had never seen the house in the country, with its barn cats and sunflower field. He thought she would, some day. There lay the fantasy.

"So now," said Tony, hitching up his summer-weight pants, "let's look at some numbers."

Down they rode in the mirrored elevator—Jill couldn't help studying her hair, which Roger would liken to a terrified cat—to the little round table and the Perrier, now flat. A tall black athlete in a dark business suit appeared from the next cubicle. "Ah!" said Tony. "Ah. This is my young colleague. Hakima Johnson. Used to play for the Pacers."

Ben squinted at the young man, who stood uncomfortably, hands folded in front of him. "I might've seen you," he said.

"I don't know," said Hakima.

"Seventy-percent free throw average, Hakkie had," said Tony. With this information, Hakima sat down. "Phenomenal," said Tony.

He began to write upside down. "Let's say you take, what? Two weeks of vacation a year?"

Ben and Jill looked at each other. Summer it had been, when Ben and his wife moved to their place by the lake. Picnic blanket under the pines. The motel by the Thruway, its flypaper and the roar of motorcycles on the access road, and salty sweat. "Two weeks, yeah," said Ben, his eyes traveling to Jill's open collar.

"Sometimes we manage a week in the winter," said Jill.

"You stay at a hotel, right?"

Making herself breathe, she pulled her eyes away. What do you do at a hotel, when you've made all the love you can make? Go for a massage. Float in the ovarian pool. Order room service. Play a game of billiards in the dark lobby, everything mute like the felt on the table. Watch Ben shoot a round of golf, his spare straight body executing the stroke, a brim shading his sharply boned face. The children, where are the children?

"Beg pardon?" she said.

"Let's say," Tony backed up patiently, "the hotel costs a hundred fifty a night, I'm being conservative, and you eat your meals out, and before you know it"—the numbers appeared right side up, left to right, for Ben and Jill—"you've shelled out three big bills for the fortnight. Am I right here?"

"You've got the math," said Ben.

"You should know, right? Numbers man," Tony clued in Hakima.

Ben touched the inside of Jill's knee. He was in the city, not just supposedly but for real, negotiating a TV script. Three or four times a year he delivered one of these, worth twenty bills, for a teenager series that was braving its way through a third season.

"Plotty," Jill had said when she'd read a couple of them.

"That's okay," Ben had said, "they like plotty."

"Plus there's the occasional weekend in New York, a place like this, count yourself another three in the hole for the year. That's six grand, flushed"—here Tony started upside-down to draw something that looked remarkably like a toilet—"down the pipes." He circled the figure and drew an arrow to the toilet bowl.

"How'd you learn to write so well upside down?" Jill asked.

"Ah now, little lady, that's a professional secret." With a flourish, Tony started the next row of figures. "You buy in here —let's say you buy in today, because today only I can give you a twenty percent reduction—for twenty-one grand for the one bedroom. That's the model you saw."

"We finance this, right?" said Ben.

"Most of our people pay cash. It's a second home, you can't write anything off, you do better to get an equity on your old place."

Hakima Johnson was drumming one leg, sending vibrations through the floorboards. He looked bored. Jill figured him for twenty-eight or twenty-nine. He hadn't made it.

She tucked the name away, to mention to Roger who would recognize if the kid really had played for the Pacers. "There I was getting my sales pitch," she'd say, "and this seven-foot trainee stepped in."

"The ninety-seven season," Roger would say, "and the guy stank."

Tony was at the upside-down numbers again. "So we are talking about either tossing six grand out every year or sinking a little over three years' worth into a place that will *make* you money. Do you have any idea what's happened to the value of a share here over the last two years? We are talking sixty percent growth. That is a gain of almost thirteen grand. More than four grand a year. So which do you like to do, my friends? Lose six thousand every year? Or make four?"

+ SIX, Tony had written in big letters on one side of the tablet of paper; - FOUR on the other.

Jill caught the eye of the former basketball player. Hakima Johnson was looking straight at her from his mink-colored eyes, and he knew. Not just that they would never in a million years buy a time-share in Manhattan Mews—even Tony Romeo, his ear dimples like cherry petals and his sweat stains grown to frisbees under his arms, knew the zero chances—but that Roger was not Roger and she was not his childless playmate, that they had betrayed everyone dear to them to come to this chintzy place and fuck like rutting goats.

Suddenly Jill was tired.

Tilting his head the way Jill imagined he tilted it when he was selling a script, Ben was finishing off the interview. Sure makes sense, he was saying, what a fabulous idea, you've got me thinking, impossible to commit today of course. Tony Romeo was asking Hakima for the form. Hakima was simply smirking, not looking at Jill anymore.

"Hey," Ben said from what seemed a great distance, "you okay?"

The blood had drained from her face; her ears rang. "I need fresh air," she said.

"Sure, sure," Tony said, pulling out a handkerchief and wiping his own brow. "The air conditioning in this place has a real temperament. We're almost done, here."

He pushed a sheet of paper forward. He had let go their balls. "This here," Tony went on, "attests to the fact that you were given this presentation, that you understood everything you were told. Now I can check here either that you're interested or that you're not interested. Either way, you get to go to the desk for your rebate and pick up your award."

"We're not interested," said Ben matter-of-factly. Upside down, Tony executed a perfect check mark. "Then I thank you both," he said, putting his palm forward, "and wish you a pleasant day."

They shook hands, all around. The basketball player's fingers lingered momentarily, but that was only because he didn't have the habit, yet, of a failed-sale handshake.

Soon, Jill and Ben were in the elevator, alone and kissing. "You were perfect, Roger," said Jill.

"*You* were prickly," Ben said.

"Roger would've been more prickly. We never would have gotten out of that waiting room. He'd have bitten Tony Romeo's head off."

"And cost you three hundred and fifty dollars." Ben's eyes began to blink. "Well, that is one difference," he said, "between Roger and me."

He was still blinking. She put a hand up, the way you would to close the eyelids on a doll. He lifted it by the wrist; smiled, puzzled. "You don't wear contacts," she said.

"What's that to do with anything?"

"You blink. You blink like your contacts were bothering you."

"Ah," he said. He pressed thumb and forefinger to his lids, then released them. "I'll try not to."

It was their first criticism, and the first trickle of cool air entered the elevator between them.

"Poor old Tony," said Ben.

"He was a prick."

"I wonder how many like us he gets."

She looked at him, puzzled. So odd, to meet eyes at the same level as hers.

"Having affairs," he said. "Looking for a trysting place."

He kissed her again, his tongue darting, and for a second in the dark elevator she saw them trysting on the beach in Hawaii, drinking pina coladas and digging their long toes into the sand. The ocean lapped; the golf course shone like plastic sheeting.

The doors opened, and Ben asked, "Which do you want?"

"Which what?"

"Which award? We get a shopping spree, dinner for two, or theatre tickets."

"Theatre tickets."

"You sure?"

"Sure. Let's see *Kiss Me, Kate*. Or that Neil Simon revival. We haven't got time to shop, and the restaurant would suck."

"Theatre, then." They were almost at the desk marked Manhattan Mews with a shared M, the little oak semicircle behind which a girl sat reading, bored. "You go to your meeting, I'll pick them up." He stopped her, his hand on her cheek, thumb on her lower lip. Tonight they would sit in upholstered seats, watching the show unroll. They wouldn't have to talk. Wouldn't have to laugh over the lies they'd told or name the places they would never travel together.

"Thank you," she said. She pressed her open hand against his crisp shirt, the tight chest underneath with its thick patch of hair. Briefly she remembered the first time she'd seen him, last summer at someone's bloated beach party, playing volleyball shirtless, leaping for the ball, a tight-muscled olive-skinned operator.

"Like your hair," he said, and his eyelids didn't blink.

"Thank you," she said again.

She felt Ben keeping something back, the thing he didn't like or wouldn't like—her dangerous brusqueness with Tony Romeo, or the way she pinched his nipple between her fingers as she came, or the sloppy linen shirts she liked to wear over her generous body. Between her legs, her muscles contracted and released. Brushing her lips against his—small, full, red, a doll's lips but warm—she turned and ran out into the bright day, the rushing traffic, the sights and sounds and smells she could take home with her. She would catch the early morning train back to Syracuse, to Roger and David and feisty Karen. She would pick up hot bagels. She would make it up to them for Hawaii, for Brittany, for the coast of Spain.

Purring

Lying awake in the bed and breakfast where they've lived for two weeks, Marcy ignites the fire. The bagel would have started smoking maybe two minutes after Ken left the house. Slowly, it would have turned black in the new white toaster (thermostatically controlled! safety first! built-in shutdown mode! DO NOT LEAVE UNATTENDED), until a spark shot out from the glowing, malfunctioning coils and a flame licked up. Crackling and spitting? She doesn't think so. Very quiet for a couple of minutes, just smoke and worms of fire eating the insides. Then something got to the plastic outside the toaster, the "cool touch" part. Upward to the base of the cupboard whooshed a topknot of flame. Then another, and a third. It would have been the third plume of fire—black smoke rising with it now, the stench of plastic burning—that lit the cupboard.

It's been so cool, and dry. A warm wet spring and now this turn in June. Should make for good corn, according to Jerry Lawless who sold Marcy all her stoneware that lies in a heap of pea-sized pieces on the floor. After bothering to put the screens up in the old windows, after listening to Ken's litany about replacing the whole batch, Marcy had finally shut all the windows and even cranked up the heat, the night before. Ken hates this climate, starts dressing in Polartec as soon as the mercury goes below fifty-five. Locals like Jerry, by contrast, are always shucking their clothes, skiing in T-shirts in February, throwing pots shirtless by May, their bare hands practically steaming in the cool air.

Anyway, Marcy thinks, the windows were closed. The double-panes in the kitchen, the heavy sashes in the mudroom. She's shifted her weight toward the edge of the B&B bed, which is way too soft. With no vent from the windows, the fire on the bottom of the china cupboard went looking for air, its little fingers poking through the wood. Meanwhile, the toaster was alight, top and bottom, and flame was beginning to burn off the polyurethane coating on the maple cabinet where the toaster sat next to Mr. Coffee and the Plexiglas cookbook holder. Marcy was always glad of that coating. She had often pointed out to Ken how nicely the drips of coffee beaded on the wood. The tall plastic containers of pasta and beans started melting, black smoke roiling up as the spaghetti spilled and burned, long matchsticks. The left half of the cupboard caught, the one with the crystal inside. Five minutes must have passed, Marcy thinks. It would have to take five, at least.

Her mother gave Marcy the china because it had been a gift from her second husband and she hated it. Pure white with a design of miniature pink and green flowers and a silver band at the rim. Doulton. Jerry Lawless has said he thinks the whole set was worth close to two thousand dollars, the most valuable thing in the kitchen. Marcy can't say she would have chosen it for herself, but then she could never imagine actually going out and choosing china for oneself. She and Ken were married in a civil ceremony and received only sporadic gifts—a leather backgammon game, a pair of Japanese prints. Only later, as other couples started giving dinner parties, did she regret not having registered, not having paid the small price of a church wedding to get all those lovely sets. The effect of her mother's china, on starched linen placemats with the crystal Ken's sister had given them, took Marcy's breath away. She never placed a piece of it in the dishwasher—the hot suds, her mother had warned, would wear away the silver trim. Not that her mother cared. She was done with that jerk. She said it made her sick to look at his plates and saucers.

Well, it hadn't made Marcy sick. This devastation made her sick, she thought as she hugged the narrow edge of the bed.

The glassware was more of a mix. Ken's sister's Dansk, which was ample and serviceable but had to have been gotten at discount, sat on the two center shelves, above the tourist-shop coffee mugs Marcy'd been collecting since college. She'd brought one of those mugs to Jerry Lawless once, for a joke, and he'd laughed at their cheap manufacture, the glued-on handles, I HEART NEW YORK.

On the top shelf were the quartet of rounded goblets that Marcy loved holding in her hand, spheres of smooth glass you never filled past halfway, with their long simple stems filtering the red color of the wine. Also, the remaining pair of Tiffany champagne glasses. Ken had bought her four of them their first Christmas together, when she didn't even think he liked her much—fluted, narrow triangles nestled in garnet red tissue, a long elegant box that she used for a while after to hold sewing notions. Six years later, their first-born, Charlie, bounced his plastic ball in the living room and knocked two of the glasses down from the display shelf. She'd even taken them to a glass repairman, a Polish Holocaust survivor in Needham, Massachusetts, where they lived then. She explained that the bases had simply been knocked off. Perhaps there was a way. "Ach yes," he said, "but look at the little crack, here, running along the curve from the top of this one. That would not hold champagne, yes?" He could fix it, he had magic ways, but we were talking seventy-five dollars per glass. And no guarantees.

For a while Marcy had kept the pieces of the broken glasses in a high cupboard, but when they moved she dumped them along with the other broken and outgrown junk. Now there are just the pair. *Were* just the pair, on the top shelf. Marcy used to bring them down with the stepladder—where was that stepladder, had it burned too?—on holidays and birthdays, the children never allowed to touch.

Caressing that left-hand cupboard, with the mugs weightiest at the bottom, the fire reached a critical point. All at once, Marcy figures from the crash Robert heard across the street, the whole contraption gave. "Like someone shooting out the windows," Robert had said. "All the windows at once."

Robert runs this B&B. He also opens the flower shop by the village green at noon. In between his tasks, he sits on his front-porch rocker waving and drinking espresso with lemon. He had seen Marcy leave the house early, then the kids running out late for school, backpacks flapping from one shoulder, Charlie's hair uncombed. But he hadn't spotted Ken. Robert had been talking to Jerry's brother, Sam Lawless, who was of all improbable things the town attorney, and they'd probably both been too wrapped up in conversation to notice Ken sprinting down the front steps, checking his watch. So Sam Lawless, when he heard breaking glass, had asked with a touch of disdain, "What *is* that Miller guy up to?" and Robert had answered loyally, "It's none of our concern!" At which point they'd seen the smoke.

So Marcy pictures the drinking things plummeting at once, crystal on top of juice glasses—the jam jars she used for the kids, only they never broke those, they broke only the good glasses, half a set gone already—on top of mugs. Plummeting to the varnished standing cupboard, now charred on top and still flaming, and then to the Italian tile. With the wall cupboard ablaze, and fire streaming across the ceiling to the cupboard above the stove, where chunks of maple fell to the floor.

A wind must have sprung up by this point, the way they say fire creates wind. The spice cabinet and the appliances cupboard (home to both the Osterizer and the Cuisinart, the tall tin of olive oil, the waffle iron, all the odd pieces of crockery—like the syrup pitcher Ken's friend Dallas had given them with its corny picture of Vermont tree-tapping—and the Godiva liqueur that Jerry gave them as a housewarming gift and that only Marcy nipped sometimes before she went up to bed) resembled a woman's carroty hair whipped by ocean breeze. Except that everywhere the kitchen was filled with black smoke, made lethal by plastic.

Marcy checks her watch, on the nightstand by the miserable bed in Robert's house. Her lower back aches. In the soft mattress, her husband's body makes a sinkhole that she's tried all night to resist. She's been thinking about the fire for a half-hour already, and by all accounts the whole thing took less than twenty-five minutes. And she hasn't even gotten to the kitchen table yet, or Jan Krupac's oil painting on the far wall that wept into a sagging waterfall of smoked color, or the cheerful clock that melted onto the wall. Of course, fire does not reflect. It consumes. Pure physics governs it, not even biology, the chance of consciousness. Still, Marcy cannot catch up to the speed of the thing.

She prepares a mental list of the things she hated. Jan's painting, for instance. Derivative Georgia O'Keeffe, woman's genitalia rendered abstract, only this time in vivid pinks and purples. Ken thought Jan was sexy when she lived across the street from them in Needham, so he'd bid on the thing at a local auction and shelled out two hundred bucks. The kids used to call it the flower picture. Recently, Charlie had decided it was a meteor exploding. Hateful also was the door to the half-bath, off the pantry, which Ken had painted himself in turquoise and bright white, supposedly to echo the color of the kitchen which was not turquoise but a very muted aqua with a hint of gray in the white tiles. And that big ugly butcher block that Ken found at a sidewalk sale. It was useful—the counter scratched so easily—but she had scrubbed at it and oiled it and scrubbed some more, and still the old scratches were the color of motor oil and the whole thing too thick and heavy for her light, water-colored kitchen.

That is, before it turned to tinder.

Be happy, everyone tells her now. Even Jerry Lawless tells her, winking. With the insurance money, you can get a brand new kitchen. You can design it just the way you want it. I had a brand new kitchen, she tells him, like a spoiled baby. I designed it. Just the way I wanted it. I want it back that way.

She can hardly bear to walk through the rubble. They can't sweep up until the claim settles, the insurance shark tells her. After everyone's taken his piece of the pie, they can start to rebuild. Whenever she picks her way through the charred piles on the wrecked floor, she picks up a shard or two, and what she loves returns. The curved side of one of those midnight blue bowls she bought from Jerry the first day she met him, for instance. Lizzy liked to fill those bowls to the brim with Rice Krispies, the white milk left afterwards inside that deep blue. Leaning on her elbow at the kitchen table, spoon in hand, Lizzie would stare absently out the window at the feeder where the yellow tanagers gathered. Eat, Marcy would remind her. You'll be late.

Always late, that Lizzy. Late that day for school, and Ken yelling at her because she couldn't find her homework, her diorama of an owl with the little mouse that Marcy had made for her out of gray clay. Late, and Ken fuming about the pots and pans, how you had to pull them out of the drawer under the oven. Ken hated putting those pots away and would always leave them on the stove for Marcy to deal with. Why couldn't they have one of those hangy things? he used to demand. There were holes in the handles of the Le Creuset, you were supposed to be able to hang the pans up, show them off.

Another item to add to the hate list. What a notion, glazed cookware. Le Creuset always stained and chipped, and you weren't allowed to bleach it for fear of taking off the finish, and the chipped places rusted. The set belonged to Ken. Marcy's been wanting Revere Ware, shiny and copper-bottomed like

Jerry Lawless has ranged along the wall of his narrow, light-flooded galley. But they will, she knows, be replacing the smoke-greased pots and casseroles with more of the same, ordered from that place in Seattle because no one carries Ken's favorite green retail any more.

She turns in the bed. Ken is stretched on his back now, his right elbow crooked and the hand placed religiously on his chest. Only by this hour, as the sky pales, does he sink into deep sleep. Thank God, she and the children tell everyone who asks, Ken was the one who left the bagel in the toaster. Any of us others would have been toast. So to speak. And the curious ones laugh and then say, But it could have happened to anyone. Sometimes, they tell their own stories, which are never so serious: a plastic cup melted onto an electric stove, a broken pot from a Mr. Coffee still on warm.

Last time through the wreckage, she picked from the stinking piles of plasterboard and blasted china a blackened shred of the Irish linen her mother had brought back from what she called her divorce trip. Marcy had stretched it and hung it above the refrigerator, where the fire must have plucked it the way the wind will pluck a dry leaf from a tree. The print on the linen was of a cat sitting contentedly. Its fur seemed calico, but on closer inspection decoded into a Gaelic saying, the letters stretched and condensed to fit the contours of the cat. IT IS FOR ITS OWN SAKE THAT THE CAT PURRS. Marcy knows the translation only by having peeked at the back. She has listed the stretched linen, along with the silver-rimmed china and the crystal and all the other unrecognizable shards, for the young shark who went around the house with a dictaphone naming contents and brand names to submit to the adjuster. She noted most objects, angrily, as being worth more than they had actually cost. The shark can battle it out with New York Mutual's casualty department, who would just as soon send them to a windowless hut in Lower Slobovia to live out their days.

Hiking up to sip stale water from the bedside glass, Marcy goes back to the flames. Slow motion, they lick across the new kitchen ceiling. Those movies that bring material things to life—*The Brave Little Toaster, Beauty and the Beast*—are on to something. She sees the hard plastic pitcher of the blender stoically fold in on itself, hears the teakettle shriek, Jerry's stoneware pray for deliverance as the smoke evaporates its finish. Finally that young woman next door, the one who's writing a dissertation on female dress code in India, opened her window to the cool morning and heard the smoke alarms. "I've always wanted to dial nine one one," the girl said when Marcy was thanking her. "I'm glad I got the chance."

The neighbors tell Ken it's not his fault. "I leave stuff like that all the time," Marcy agrees. Truth is, Marcy has never in her life put something into the toaster and walked out the door. Sleepless mornings like this, her back raw and Robert's sugary voice below, singing old Frank Sinatra, she comforts herself with Ken's guilt.

"Built his kitchen," one of those same neighbors said to Jerry Lawless, "and then burned it down himself."

In the soft bed, Ken turns onto his left side, flinging his arm over his head just the way Charlie does. Like Charlie's, his face hides nothing—even in sleep, she can trace the mark of the fire in the heaviness of his brow and the newly protective hunch of his loose shoulders. Her face and Lizzy's face, on the other hand, drop down like shutters over whatever they don't want the world to see. The bed quakes with Ken's turning. Marcy gathers the thin white coverlet and takes to the thickly carpeted floor, where she's ended up four of the last five mornings.

On the floor, when she's lucky, she sinks into deep vivid dreams, mostly of travel, exotic marketplaces and the anxiety of missed trains. This morning, though, the sun is already filtering through Robert's bamboo blinds and the kids will be awake soon, slipping into the upstairs sitting room where they can gobble up cartoons. So no dreams, but at least the floor keeps still.

It doesn't matter, she repeats to herself as she shuts her eyes against the yellow daylight, where she was or what she was doing when Ken learned the news and came tearing back from his little office in the village. She had put it on the calendar a full week before: MARCY LEAVE 8 A.M. Early meeting, she had explained. She had earned the privilege, earned it many times over. And she might well have had an early meeting. What difference would it have made to the outcome if she had? How many times had Ken left early for one reason or another, and she got the kids out to school without burning the kitchen down?

Still, from the floor, she sees herself reaching lazily for the phone by Jerry Lawless's bed and dialing in for her voicemail. The pleasant recorded woman's voice telling her she has one new message, and then Ken's voice, tight and sad with the tidings.

He will never say to her, if you had not gone to meet your lover, the children would have got off calmly to school and no one would have forgotten a bagel in the toaster, and we would have our home still. He will never say it because he will never know. And she will not bear his guilt. When his guilt comes to her like this, with the moving picture of Jerry fucking her slowly, his pot-throwing fingers deep between her buttocks, his mouth at her ear, the light from the cheap blinds playing over their twined legs—when Ken's guilt comes to her like this, she refuses it.

She may yet cause many things to happen. But she did not cause fire to leap up and sweep away her kitchen. She wants anyone passing judgment to be clear, at least on that point. On the carpeted floor in the early morning, it seems clear enough to her.

The Woman Who Said No

He was putting on his shoes when he told her. "Samantha wants a contract."

"A what?"

"Contract. Or something. She wants me to write something down."

"What kind of something down?"

"It should say that if I ever have sex with someone else again, our marriage is over."

They were both sitting on the edge of the motel bed. "And you said?"

"I'd think about it."

Marian traced the print on the bedspread. It made a complicated geometric pattern, like Rubik's cube or a pair of those twisted nails that should come apart easily but don't. "How long do you have to think?"

"I don't know. She came up with the idea last week."

Marian ran her finger down Joe's back, lithe and muscled under the slippery cotton of his shirt. A quarter of an hour ago she had lain behind him, curled on the bed, and thought how similar one back looks to another—shoulder blades, trapezoids, the knotty rope of spine. That she was not Joe's first affair was part of his attractiveness for her: she needn't take him too seriously. "Well," she said, draping her arm over Joe's narrow shoulder, like an old friend, "that's really between you and

Samantha, isn't it?"

"Yeah, I suppose it is. I shouldn't bother you with it."

"But if you sign a contract and keep seeing me, you'll be in deep trouble," said Marian.

"I'm already in deep trouble."

"I think I'd want to break off, if there was a contract on file." Marian drew away, was sitting cross-legged on the bed. "Then again, if you refuse to sign it, she'll know you're up to something."

"That about sums up the possibilities."

Joe smiled, and Marian touched a lean dimple on his cheek. "So what are you going to do?"

"Stall. What would you do, Counselor?"

Marian stood and began to dress. She was a tall, thin, freckled woman with gluteal muscles far sexier, she thought, than her slight breasts. For that reason, she kept her back to Joe as she slipped back into skirt, bra, blouse, hose.

"She doesn't mean to catch you," she said, her eyes on the ray of December light that slipped between the heavy maroon curtains. Joe had picked this motel, a cheap all-season place up a winding road at the New Hampshire border. "If she wants you to sign a contract like that, it means she's expecting you to be tempted, right?"

"She knows," said Joe, shaking out a sock, "that monogamy is not my strong suit."

"But she's also thinking you would tell her about it. Given the signed contract. And that by choosing to tell her, you'd be choosing to end your marriage. Which isn't at all, I think"—she turned around, her blouse half buttoned, and leaned over him to smell his curly hair—"what you're doing here. With me."

He didn't answer. He made her take her clothes back off, so that she was late, and messy, that day getting back to work. And though she believed that what Joe wrote down for his wife was no business of hers, Marian Lewis was a lawyer and knew the ins and outs of contracts, the loopholes and the parsing of phrases, so the subject wouldn't quite move off her agenda.

She had met Joe at a party in Boston. No, not quite. First, he had come up to Peterborough to report on the state senator's fabulous divorce. He had returned to check facts. Then, in November, Marian had driven her daughter, Lisa, to Boston for sectional finals—girls' 14-and-under tennis—and stolen away from the match to a cocktail party, and there he had been, popping baby quiches into his mouth like a starving man.

There was always the chance she might have said no. The other times she had, in so many words, said no. Instead, under the ficus tree in the Boston loft, she had been the one to kiss Joe—on his neck, under his right ear. If she hadn't, he'd have kissed her. Or tried to. But she could have said no, and then he wouldn't have tried again. Sometimes, sitting in conference or driving through late-winter snow, Marian pictured herself saying no. Suddenly it was as if she were living parallel lives, the life in which she'd said yes and the life in which she'd said no. And the lives were so much alike, even she had trouble telling them apart. Like those pairs of pictures in the puzzle books the children used to read, where you strain to find the ten differences between the pictures.

"Sometime you'll have to tell me," Joe had said, lying naked next to her on the motel bed near the state border, "what you are doing here."

"I was hoping you'd tell me," she said, and blew on his chest, which had a thicker mat of hair than her husband Edward's and smelled like salted butter.

Throughout that winter, Marian carried her affair inside her like a secret taint of blood. It came to her at odd moments, like when she'd dropped her son, Kurt, off for hockey and was on her way through wet snow to the mall. Turning the corner at the light she'd think, I'm fucking a man not my husband, and a little rush would come between her legs.

Sometimes, it would not come, and there were only the words, I'm fucking a man, so that Marian could consider them there in the slowly lightening days. I'm involved with someone outside my marriage, she tried sometimes. She liked the way that sounded—as a line she might use on someone she was confessing to, if she were ever to confess—but she preferred to remind herself that what she was doing was fucking Joe.

The terrible thing, if she could find nothing wrong enough in her marriage to justify adultery, was that she was there out of frivolity. She did it because she got away with it. Or worse, she did it in the hope that Joe would fall in love with her, would leave his pretty zoologist wife for her, would work to persuade her to leave Edward.

And of course she wasn't going to leave Edward, so this hope was mere vanity.

Marian had never been a pretty woman. She had set her sights on Edward because of his beauty—his nose alone gave him the edge over Joe, who was snappy-looking at best—and because he sang. A lovely, dark chocolate baritone. Songs from *Camelot* and *West Side Story*; he'd sung "Maria" to her on their first date, in law school, though her name was Marian and others had sung to her about the librarian. Even now, he told her all the time how beautiful she was. Her small neat ass, her milky breasts, her slim hips and long waist. After fourteen years he remarked with wonder on what others might have called a stringy figure.

Joe never told her she was beautiful; he did not believe, she surmised, that she was. He only fucked her, and with such grace and urgency that she could not think of anything else while they were at it.

She had to be careful not to transfer Joe's style of lovemaking over to Edward. For instance, if she put the tips of her

fingers into Edward's mouth for him to suck while she was strad-
dling him, he'd have stopped what he was doing, torn her wrist
away from her face, and stared a confession out of her. Or if
she'd let him put a finger into her anus, the way he used to want
to and she'd never let him. She let Joe do anything.

Joe was an investigative reporter. Murders he covered, generally, also gruesome auto accidents and political scandals. He'd
interviewed Marian in the first place because she represented
the senator in his bid for divorce. They discussed the ethics of
prenuptial agreements, the ethics of politics, the lawyer-client
privilege, the ethics of marrying money. In retrospect, Marian
thought, they'd both come off as remarkably ethical people.

"What if you wrote," she tried the next time she arranged
to meet Joe, at a ski resort where he was investigating a crime
of passion committed by the cook, "that infidelity on your part
would be grounds for divorce? There's a lot of wiggle room in
'grounds.'"

He tried to grin, but it didn't last. They were drinking
Scotch, which he always brought along. Marian had been lining up their legs, which were almost exactly the same length,
only Joe's more muscled and dark with hair. "That's like Clinton
dismissing oral sex," he said, swirling his drink. "It could squeak
by in court but not in anyone's conscience."

"I haven't come up with much else."

He put his hand, the one with the ring, on her thigh,
rubbed a damp spot with his thumb. "It's not your job to,
Counselor," he said.

There would be nothing legally binding about it, of course.
Joe could write, *Evidence that I am having an affair with another
woman will mean the end of our marriage.* He could write, *On
learning that Joe is having sex with another woman, Samantha may
choose to end the marriage.* Samantha would spot the slippery
language in both those versions. Their condition was the affair's

coming to light, not the affair itself, and the second one put the burden of proof on Samantha.

This marriage will continue only on the condition that neither partner has sex with anyone outside the marriage. The second his penis penetrated Marian, Joe's marriage would end. Would he then need to rush home and tell Samantha that their union had ruptured? Could the end of a marriage be one partner's secret?

Marian began to consider Samantha a very clever woman. She was relying on Joe's faithfulness, not to her, but to the words he set down on the page.

Twice in January Marian saw Joe, and they didn't mention the contract. Meeting Joe could be tricky business. He drove up her way on short notice, following the news, whereas her day was tightly booked. Marian handled what she labeled "price-tag divorces." It wasn't the prettiest field of law, negotiating settlements between people worth seven figures each, but because these people enjoyed the privilege of contacting their attorney at home, she was likewise able to construct a flexible schedule for herself. Her assistant, Pearl, who had grown children, was sensitive to Marian's need to keep tabs. If she started out of the office without mentioning where she was headed, Pearl was sure to pull out her notepad. "You'll be in range?" she'd say. "You won't forget your four o'clock? Sure you don't want me to have that material faxed?" The surprising thing, Marian sometimes thought, was not that she was morally willing to commit adultery, but that she had the brain power left over to concoct the appropriate excuses.

After the second winter rendezvous, two months went by with nothing but e-mails. Joe was covering a murder trial on Cape Cod, a fisherman who'd strangled his boss with fishing twine and thrown him overboard in a net. It was bleak on the Cape. His wife wanted him to drive home every night, ninety miles. *What about the contract?* Marian wrote. Meaning, did he have another lover on the Cape?

We're working on wording, Joe wrote. *If it weren't for you,* he wrote, *I'd have no problem with the thing.*

Meaning he had no other woman, at the moment. Marian found herself grinning as she drove Lisa to practice.

"What's so funny, Mom?" Lisa asked. She was a muscular girl who resembled her father; when she lost a match, which she did often enough, she sucked in her lower lip for a long minute, then shrugged her shoulders and flipped her racquet up.

"Nothing, honey. Just something someone at work said."

"What? Is it a joke?"

"Sort of. A grown-up joke."

"You can tell me," said Lisa. "Dad lets me watch *Seinfeld.*"

"No." Marian worked hard to straighten her mouth. "It's not that funny, really."

Things are better at home, Joe wrote when the Cape Cod trial was over. He was looking for an assignment in New Hampshire. Maybe she had some legal business in Boston?

Did you ever sign that contract? she wrote.

In reply he wrote a very long funny e-mail about a man who'd been caught slaughtering pigs on his balcony in South Boston and selling the meat. He tacked on a P.S. to say that he missed her hands on his ass and another P.S. to note that things were still pretty smooth at home. Meaning that Samantha had decided to drop the contract idea.

Well, it was a stupid idea. Judging from Marian's clients, if you had to resort to a legal document beyond a marriage license to keep your husband from straying, you might as well forget the whole thing.

Of course, Marian didn't know Samantha. Joe had allowed that Samantha worked with large cold-blooded animals at the Boston Zoo. She was competent and affectionate, Marian gathered, and came home stinking of snake. Which did not seem to be the source of Joe's compulsive infidelity, though surely it didn't help. Marian pictured Samantha as all the things she wasn't:

small, rounded, fair, faithful. Lying awake next to Edward, she thought of Joe's loose, almost hairless testicles resting against his wife's plump thigh.

Spring arrived early in New Hampshire. Mud season came and went in a week. The streams swelled. Crocus gave way almost instantly to tulips and daffodils, and the trees leafed out dangerously. Edward's schedule—he was a tax attorney, mostly for small business—picked up, and Marian cut back to help more at home. By April, despite the e-mails and a couple of office phone calls, she had almost become the woman who had said no. Lisa persuaded her to come pound balls on the town courts as soon as the thermometer went above forty degrees. Kurt broke his arm falling from his bike in the muddy slush, and Edward spent his evenings helping his son write left-handed homework. When the kids were in bed, Marian and Edward spread out a map of the Canadian Rockies and started sketching a plan that involved summer backpacking and sightings of moose. "Younger than springtime are you," Edward sang when she won the state senator's case. "Gayer than laughter are you. Warm as the winds of June are the gentle lips you gave me."

Edward's face was a flawless oval, his ears small, his nose so sharp and firm it seemed to lack cartilage. Approaching to kiss her, he held his mouth slightly open, his tongue already at his lips, so that she thought of being licked by a dog. "Please," she giggled at the song.

"Please what? What can I do to please my brilliant wife? Would you like a nice slow backrub? My hands on your delectable thighs? Hm?"

As if it had happened to a close friend, Marian remembered making love with a man who never praised, never asked how he might please her, who created pleasure with the force of his desire. "Everything you do," she said to Edward, injecting a sultry tone, "makes me feel nice."

The next week her computer brought a note from Joe. He'd landed an assignment, he wrote. A utilities scandal up by Bristol. He would be leaving in the morning, a two-day trip. Did that give her enough time?

She wrote back that she would think of something. And assigned that task to the woman who had said yes, while she went on with the day's work.

That night, the rain started late and changed over to sleet in the small hours. Edward took the kids to school—Kurt holding his plastered arm close to his chest as if the sleet would dissolve it, Lisa lugging her racquet. "Be careful!" Marian called to them.

"This sucks," said Kurt.

"Be over in a day," said Marian.

"In Florida," said Lisa, "they're wearing halters by now."

"In Florida," said Edward, "tax lawyers are the earth's scum."

"So do divorce," said Lisa.

"And leave your lovely mother? Perish the thought," said Edward.

"Dad, I meant—" started Lisa, but then she saw him wink at Marian. "Jesus, let's go," she said.

Whistling "April, Come She Will," Edward fitted on his sunglasses, a perverse trick he always pulled when the weather turned gray, as if to fool himself into thinking that the shades were what made the day gloomy. Marian didn't remark. She didn't like to talk much, when she was going to see Joe. Each phrase, each bit of daily business was an ill-fitting disguise. Breathing, she felt a bubble at the center of her chest.

Then her family was gone from the street, and she pulled together papers, snapped off the coffee machine, and took herself to work as if the only disturbance in the day were the stuff coming from the sky. From the office, she phoned Joe at the *Globe*. "Just making sure," she said.

"Weather's lousy, I hear," he said.

"An indoor day." She tried to make her voice sound suggestive, but instead was reminded of a playground aide, planning recess.

"We can check in at that little motel," he said, "at two o'clock."

"The one in the mountains? Is it open?"

"Eager for our business," he said. And then, dropping his voice, "Samantha's on again. About the contract."

"Oh, dear." She sat at her desk. "I haven't come up with a good solution to that," she said. "Have you signed anything?"

"Not—well, not really. I've been fiddling with it."

"So bring what you've been fiddling with. I'm a lawyer, I *do* contracts. Maybe we can find something you can live with. I mean, not that I care. But it's important to you."

"Thanks," he said. He sounded edgy.

"So we're still on."

"Oh, yeah. Yeah. As close to two as I can make it."

They hung up. Marian's hands were sweating. She rose and went to the window of her office—six stories up, the highest building in Peterborough. Before, when she had arranged to meet Joe, the confirming phone call had resembled foreplay. She'd known already what her alibi was. She'd been living her day, already, as though the Marian who was *not* having an affair really *was* going to the law library in Keene or the coffeehouse in Exeter. The Marian who spoke with Joe just before meeting him was usually the shadow Marian, the one who'd said *yes* and not *no*. Today, though, the sleet had spoiled things. Today, the Marian who had said no had answered the phone, had made the arrangement as if it were an item on the schedule Pearl so carefully kept.

She spent the morning on the phone with an attorney in Portsmouth, hammering out details of a custody arrangement between an airline pilot and his pediatrician wife. She represented the husband, who wanted weekends, summers, and holidays; the wife wanted Christmas. The children were two, four, and five. She stayed in for lunch. Outside, it had begun to sleet again, the daffodils bending under the weight. Joe was driving north by now. Edward was tucked into his home office, humming through the numbers. At ten minutes past one Marian left a note on Pearl's desk: *Gone shopping, back by four.* She would forget her cell phone. People did, sometimes. They wandered off, they got distracted. Such was the stuff of which movies were made. Marian had always worried, under the surface, about the jobs and families and ordinary futures of the characters in movies, whose lives seemed to happen only when they slacked off.

But she could explain it all away, for this one time.

Ice had crusted on the car. She stood toe-deep in slush in spring shoes and scraped. Around her in the parking lot, people hugged their thin coats, hoisted umbrellas. In the car, she turned on both heat and defrost, and waited until warm air was blasting her wet toes, then she pulled out of the lot and headed east. She had expected, she realized as she paused at the first light, to be stopped—to run into a client, or Pearl asking what on earth she meant, shopping in this weather. *Why, Marian, you never shop!*

The sleet changed over to rain, then back to sleet. Cars were fishtailing in the fast lane. Marian flicked the windshield wipers onto double time, like snake tails lashing. The defrost blew at top heat; the air in the car was like a desert. Here and there cars had pulled over, their drivers huddled inside or seeking shelter at one of the taverns along the way. Bushes in full bloom dragged on the ground like dresses tossed aside. At the Allenbury exit she turned onto Oxbow Road, which wound around a long hill toward the motel. This was what you did. You drove ridiculous distances in awful weather to fuck in a cheap motel and give flimsy excuses about it later. Oh, she loved it. Joe with his sharp chin, Joe with his hand making her damp before she could get her clothes off. The car climbed. The Marian who had said no dropped behind.

And yet. If Edward had asked her. If he had said—which he never would, because he would never know—but if he had said, "Write me a contract," she would have written it. In five minutes. And called Joe. And said, "It is over." Who waited for such things? Who could sign such things and go on with the betrayal?

The motel smelled of coffee and carpet cleaner, the lobby so poorly lit that at first she didn't see Joe, lounging by the Hostess Bar with a styrofoam cup. "Hey, beautiful," he called in a low voice.

"Where's your car? Am I late?"

"Around back. No."

"I left my cell phone at the office."

"Clever girl."

She'd approached him and now they kissed, each of them tipping their faces exactly the same amount. Joe had put the cup down and slipped that warm hand under Marian's raincoat to her waist. He was wearing reporter's clothes, brown leather jacket and loose-weave shirt. "So what's this case?" she asked him.

"Tell you later." He had her hips pulled to him; she could feel his erection. With his free hand he brought forth a slim plastic card. "Room two-oh-four," he said. "Same as before."

"Poet," she said. And tried not to be embarrassed by the oblique stare of the small, neatly coiffed woman behind the reception desk as they mounted the stairs at the back of the lobby.

They made love quickly, the first time. Marian had worn clothes easy to remove, and their bodies coupled as though making sure they still fit. Joe brought out the Scotch and fetched plastic glasses from the bathroom. She liked to watch him move, from behind—the fine set of his hips, his small bare feet. She had come, but so quickly that it seemed an accident, and in her mind's eye she still saw the sleet battering her windshield, the tire marks of skidders on the road. "So tell," she said when they'd clicked cups, the plastic only whispering, "about the contract."

"There's not much to tell." He smiled his roguish smile.

"You didn't bring anything?"

"No."

"You said she was on about it."

"She's been anxious." He stroked the thin coverlet. "I'm gone so much. We talked about my changing over to editorial."

The Scotch burned down Marian's throat. Water, that's what she'd really like. "You signed it," she guessed. "Didn't you?"

"No!" He swallowed his Scotch, a little too quickly she thought. "Haven't even got the wording hammered out. That's not so important, anyway."

He put his plastic cup down on the pressed-board side table and moved lower on the bed. Taking her foot in his hands, he began to massage the ball and arch. As he bent his head, she could see a bald spot the size of a poker chip. Marian leaned back against the headboard.

"That trial on Cape Cod," he was saying, "was about the bottom of the barrel. I mean, the murderer was schizoid. He should have been in the mental health system a decade ago. And they were all dirt-poor and alcoholic except the Hispanics, who aren't really fisherman. They're cocaine runners. I felt slimed, just covering the thing. Knocking out the sensationalist prose, getting it in under the word count." He moved his hands to her Achilles tendon, stretched her calf muscles. "I've got to change my life, Marian," he said.

She was only half-listening. The foot felt delicious; the other one waited eagerly for its turn. But something wasn't right. "The contract," she said again. "I mean, are we really talking about a contract?"

He looked up at her, sort of dreamily. "Don't be a lawyer," he said.

She shut her eyes. He was doing her toes, now. When he'd done both feet, they would make love again, more slowly and with greater intent. If Joe was lying, if he had signed a contract, he might have done it yesterday or last week—or last fall even, before they began. He'd meant to break it to her slowly, because he wasn't ready to give her up yet. For Joe, a contract with Samantha would imply—for no good and certainly no legal reason—a certain grace period. Before the conditions actually locked in. By the end of, say, May, when he was prepared to part from Marian, he would admit to having signed the thing.

On the other hand. He'd taken up the left foot now, thank God, his thumb on the arch. On the other hand, there may have been no contract at all. Neither requested nor proffered. He mentioned such things to women to give himself an escape hatch. When he was ready to end the affair, he counted on his co-conspirator's sense of decency. The minute he claimed he'd actually signed the contract, whichever woman he was with would feel obliged to break off.

"You can tell me you signed it," she said, her eyes shut. "I won't ask about wording."

"Jesus, Marian. Can you just stop about the contract?"

"It's not my contract."

"*Exactly*. I'm trying to tell you something else."

He was, too. Ever since the phone call yesterday, Joe had been trying to tell her something else. Only it was sleeting outside, bending the newly leafed branches, and they might let school out early, and her husband would sing to her, and what was she doing here?

"I can't say yes," said Marian. Unexpectedly her eyes filled with tears.

"I haven't even asked yet," said Joe. He'd let go her feet, was kissing her legs, moving upward. She reached for her Scotch, finished it.

"I need a drink of water," she said.

"In a minute." He was at her belly now, nipping the tender skin with his teeth.

"I'd rather," she said, letting him pull her flat on the bed, "that there be a contract."

"I'm going to ask you," he murmured against her skin, "to change your life with me."

"I told you. I can't say yes."

"I haven't asked yet."

He turned her over onto her belly. Against the warm sheets she felt all the places he'd nipped her, buzzing. He moved down and licked between her buttocks. She looked at the wide low window—they hadn't drawn curtains, nothing but woods outside—where sleet still flung itself. Lisa, she thought. Kurt. Edward. As if they were out there somewhere, slogging through the cold muck, the downed branches. People she knew, who knew her, the other Marian. Then Joe's penis was between her buttocks, his hand on her breast.

"No," she said.

"It's new for me, too," he said. She heard for the first time the fear in his voice. His cock pushed forward a little. She clenched, then released, and the tip of his shaft entered her.

She was fucking Joe. Joe was fucking her. There either was a contract or there wasn't. She would let him do anything, those were the terms. It made no difference, no obvious difference, in the rest of her life. Marian repeated these phrases to herself while Joe kissed her between her shoulder blades. Then he pushed in further, and began moving.

She groaned. She didn't form any words. His hand moved down, between her legs, and one finger went inside her where his cock wasn't, while the others moved among the folds of her labia, her clitoris. He pushed his penis in farther, moving, really fucking her there now, and a queer taste came in her mouth, and she wasn't even sure she was Marian any more, and with a shock she came. Only then, after a few more thrusts, did he pull out—he had gone deeper than she thought—and spilled warm across her lower back, with a catch in his throat as he let go, and his gamey fingers in her mouth where her lips held them.

They lay hot on the white sheets. After a minute, Joe rose and went again to the bathroom, and came back with a plastic cup filled with water. Marian drank, the taste still in her throat. Then she lay on her back. On Joe's thigh, her hand barely trembled. He was not handsome, she thought. His face wore its lines hard. In late middle age he would take to combing hair over his bald spot, giving attention to his sloping forehead, his hook nose, the creases in his neck.

"I don't have an assignment in New Hampshire," he said. "I wrote a contract and then tore it up. I've left Samantha."

Marian didn't say anything. Clumsily, propped on an elbow, she finished off the water. If *left* meant *kicked out by*, there was nothing in Joe's Scotch-roughened voice (he would never sing to her) that called his innocent, clever wife to account. Raising herself up, she put her arms around Joe. There was no difference between his smell and hers, both of them violated and rank and intimate.

"Did I hurt you?" he asked.

Against his shoulder Marian shook her head, but then had to say it. "No, Joe," she said.

"No what?"

He was a person now, to her. That was the awful part. "You didn't hurt me," she confessed. And felt with the danger of a spring storm how she would drive back down the mountain, tires slipping, unable to resist the sleeted road that ran between *no* and *yes*.